CLASS
TRiP CHAOS

STORY LINK®
PROGRAM

"Saved by the Bell" titles include:

Mark-Paul Gosselaar: Ultimate Gold

Mario Lopez: High-Voltage Star

Behind the Scenes at "Saved by the Bell"

Beauty and Fitness with "Saved by the Bell"

▲ ▼ ▲

Hot new fiction titles:

Zack Strikes Back

Bayside Madness

California Scheming

Girls' Night Out

Zack's Last Scam

Class Trip Chaos

CLASS TRIP CHAOS

by Beth Cruise

Collier Books
Macmillan Publishing Company
New York

Maxwell Macmillan Canada
Toronto

Maxwell Macmillan International
New York   Oxford   Singapore   Sydney

Collier Books   Maxwell Macmillan Canada, Inc.
Macmillan Publishing Company   1200 Eglinton Avenue East
866 Third Avenue   Suite 200
New York, NY 10022   Don Mills, Ontario M3C 3N1

Macmillan Publishing Company is part of the Maxwell
Communication Group of Companies.

First Collier Books edition 1992
Printed in the United States of America

10   9   8   7   6   5   4   3   2

ISBN 0-02-042765-4
LC Number: 92-35523

To
"Saved by the Bell"
fans everywhere

Chapter 1

▲ ▼ ▲ ▼ ▲ ▼ ▲

Zack Morris pressed his face against the airplane window and stared down at the chrome-and-steel skyline of New York City. "Watch out, Manhattan," he crowed. "The Bayside High seniors are about to invade!"

Zack's girlfriend, Kelly Kapowski, leaned toward him. "Look, they're boarding up the windows," she said, giggling. "They must have heard about you, Zack."

Zack's hazel eyes twinkled, and his smile tilted into his trademark devilish grin. It was true—he *was* considered the biggest troublemaker at Bayside High in Palisades, California. But on the class trip, he'd already decided to lay low. It was the decent thing to do. Besides, Mr. Belding, the principal of Bayside High, had warned him that if he heard one *whisper* of trouble about Zack from the chaperones, he'd give him detention until graduation.

"Kelly, haven't I promised that this will be seven scam-free days?" Zack asked.

"Sure," Kelly agreed, flipping a lock of long, silky dark hair over her shoulder. Her blue eyes sparkled with amusement. "But that doesn't mean I believe it."

Kelly was the prettiest girl at Bayside High, but that didn't mean she wasn't smart. She also happened to be the *nicest* girl at Bayside, but she was no pushover. She had Zack's number, all right.

Zack put on a hurt expression. "Gosh, Kelly. That hurts. I look at myself as an *ambassador*. We're representing the honor of old Bayside High. Be true to your school, Kelly. I, for one, am going to uphold the honor and integrity of our illustrious forebears—"

Suddenly, a head full of springy, wild curls popped over the seat in front of them. "You saw four bears?" Samuel "Screech" Powers asked. "Wow. We must be passing over the Bronx Zoo."

"In that case, maybe you should parachute down, Screech," Zack responded.

"No way. I haven't finished my peanuts yet." Screech slid back down in his seat.

Zack had known Screech all his life, and he was just beginning to suspect that Screech was not a person at all. He was just a long, bony bundle of nerve endings with a brain attached. And sometimes Zack wasn't even *positive* about the brain.

Kelly leaned over to look out the window at the impressive Manhattan skyline. "It's beautiful," she said. "But it looks kind of big and scary, too."

Zack smelled the fresh lemon scent of Kelly's silky hair as she leaned against him. He sighed in happiness. His mission on this class trip was simple: seven days of up-close and personal contact with his sweetie.

"Don't worry, Kelly," he said as she leaned back in her seat. "I'll be spending every minute with you. Long walks in Central Park, romantic dinners in out-of-the-way French restaurants, dancing—"

"Whoa, hold on," Kelly said, laughing. "Mr. Loomis has practically every day and night full of scheduled activity. Don't you remember the mimeographed handout we all got when we boarded the plane?"

"Are you kidding?" Zack said with a groan. "It added five pounds to my carry-on luggage. We must be visiting every single historical site in New York City."

Mr. Loomis was a strict history teacher at Bayside, and he was using this class trip as his opportunity to cram even more obscure historical facts down the students' throats.

"And when we're not touring historical spots,

we'll be in museums," Kelly said with a sigh. "Ms. McCracken made sure of that. I wonder if we'll be able to have any fun at all."

"Don't worry, we will," Zack assured her. "I'm going to make sure of it. I have a plan."

Kelly's dark blue eyes narrowed suspiciously. "Whatever happened to that scam-less seven days you promised me?"

"I didn't say I had a *scam*," Zack said innocently. "I said I have a *plan*."

"For you, a plan *is* a scam," Kelly said.

"Actually, it's more like a good deed," Zack replied. "Look down there in the first row. What do you see?"

Kelly gave a quick glance down the aisle, then leaned back against her seat again. "Mr. Loomis and Ms. McCracken are ignoring each other. He's reading some thick, boring book and she's sketching. So?"

Zack made a buzzing noise. "Wrong, Ms. Kapowski. You do *not* win the deluxe double-door refrigerator. Care to try for the trash compactor?"

Kelly crinkled her adorable nose at him. "Zack, what are you talking about?"

"Okay, let me tell you what you *actually* see," Zack explained. "Mr. Loomis and Ms. McCracken—two lonely people made for each other who are afraid to make contact. As soon as Willard Loomis and Maisie McCracken realize that they're in love, we'll have our freedom."

"Mr. Loomis and Ms. McCracken?" Kelly felt Zack's forehead. She clucked her tongue. "What a shame, getting delirious on the first day of our class trip."

"Kelly, I'm serious," Zack said.

Kelly sighed. "That's what scares me."

"Wait, Kelly. You have to admit that Mr. Loomis is handsome in a stuffy kind of way. And Ms. McCracken is cute." Zack ticked off the items on his fingers. "They're about the same age, they have teaching in common, and they both work all the time."

"But they're total opposites!" Kelly protested. "Mr. Loomis wears button-down shirts and suits. Even on the class trip, he's wearing a tie. I can tell what kind of woman he'll fall for. Some blond former deb with little pearl earrings and an A-line dress."

"How do you know that?" Zack asked. "I don't even know what an A-line dress *is*."

"I'm a girl, that's how," Kelly said firmly. "Look at Ms. McCracken. Her earrings look like percussion instruments for some Amazon tribe. Her hair isn't just red—it's orange. She's always wearing flowing scarves and skirts. I'm telling you, she's not his type."

"You're talking about appearances," Zack said. "They don't matter, really."

"Okay," Kelly said. "How about personalities? Mr. Loomis is always talking about 'the bottom line' and 'getting down to brass tacks.' Meanwhile, Ms. McCracken is telling us to 'free our creative potential' and do 'serious sharing.' On Mr. Loomis's last vacation, he went to the British Museum to read all of Queen Victoria's correspondence. Ms. McCracken went to the top of Mount Rainier to get in touch with her inner child."

"So they're a little different," Zack said. "They'll broaden each other's horizons."

"Oh, there's one more thing I forgot to point out," Kelly continued. "They hate each other's guts."

Zack clucked his tongue. "You're so negative, Kelly. So they have a few differences of opinion. Big deal."

"A few! They practically screamed at each other at the planning meeting for the trip. Remember Ms. McCracken telling Mr. Loomis that she had a news flash for him—the twentieth century has arrived? And did you see Ms. McCracken's face when Mr. Loomis asked *her* if her college major was finger painting?"

"You see? Sparks!" Zack said. "Love will find a way. I just have to help it along. By Sunday, love will be in full bloom. Today's Monday—this afternoon, I'll give the first teeny push."

"Try a bulldozer," Kelly answered.

"That's Wednesday's plan," Zack said composedly.

▲   ▼   ▲

One row ahead of Zack and Kelly, Lisa Turtle placed her last letter on the travel Scrabble board. *"L-O-V-E,"* she spelled out. "And the *V* is on a triple letter score. That should give me—"

"Seventy-five points all together," Screech said. "I still win. You *could* have won, Lisa, if you had been paying more attention. Just look at your words!" Screech looked down at the tiny Scrabble board. "Romance. Hug. Sweetheart. Soccer?"

Lisa's pretty face grew dreamy. "Cal plays soccer," she said. "You should see him bounce that little white ball off his head. He's adorable."

Screech sighed. Cal Everhart was Lisa's new boyfriend. They'd only been dating a week, and she was already head over heels.

"Gosh," Screech complained, "for a minute there, I thought we'd make it through a conversation without bringing up Cal."

It wasn't that he didn't want Lisa to be happy. But he wanted her to be happy with *him.* Lisa was a beautiful, vivacious African-American teen, and he had had a crush on her since he'd seen her in that little yellow playsuit when she was seven. She had the sweetest smile this side of heaven. If Cal broke her heart, Screech would break his face. Or maybe he'd get their muscular friend, A. C. Slater, to break his face. But he'd be on the sidelines, cheering.

"I can't help it, Screech," Lisa said as she closed up the Scrabble board. "I just miss him so much."

"It's only the first day of the trip," Screech pointed out.

"I know," Lisa said mournfully. "It's agony. If only Cal's parents hadn't planned that family reunion in Colorado. I could be spending seven whole days with him!"

Just then, Screech saw a light brown eye pressed against the crack of the seat in front of him. He recognized the greedy gaze of Nanny "Nosy" Parker, who wrote the gossip column for the *Bayside Beacon*, the school paper. She was obviously trying to eavesdrop on him and Lisa, and that meant trouble.

Nanny had *already* written about Screech in her column and humiliated him in front of the whole school. She had printed that he was practically suicidal because of Lisa's crush on Cal. That was bad enough. Then she had to print in black and white that Screech had never had a girlfriend! She had blown his image as a stud, and Screech would never forgive her. He was sure that his macho image would have gotten him a date sooner or later.

Screech had been so embarrassed that he'd done a stupid thing. He'd invented a girlfriend for two whole weeks. The only one who had known that Crystal was a figment of his imagination had been Lisa. She knew him so well that she'd guessed the truth, and he could never lie to Lisa.

"Shhh," he told Lisa warningly. He winked at her and rolled his eyes toward the seat in front of them.

But Lisa only sighed. "Oh, Screech, you just don't get it. You don't understand what it's like to miss someone. You've never been in love. You've never had a steady girlf—"

Suddenly, Screech faked a coughing fit. Then he started winking furiously and rolling his eyes around even more frantically.

"What's the matter?" Lisa asked. "Do you have something in your eye, or are you having a seizure?"

Screech pointed to his nose.

"You have something in your nose?" Lisa asked doubtfully.

Exasperated, Screech pointed to his nose again and then to the seat in front of them. This time, Lisa got it.

"Except for Crystal, of course," she said in a louder tone. "I know you were really heartbroken when that didn't work out."

Screech sniffed. "My heart *was* broken."

"You should take the same consolation I do, Screech," Lisa said. "Remember that we're heading for one of the greatest shopping capitals of the world. I can't wait to hit the stores! All I need is the magic word."

"What's the magic word?" Screech asked. Lisa was renowned over three counties for her shopping ability. He wouldn't be surprised if they declared Lisa Turtle Day at the mall.

"Sale," Lisa said dreamily. "Now, just look at this purse." She held up her petite pink leather purse in front of Screech. "This is at *least* a three-day project. I have to replace it because the catch keeps coming open. It's going to take time to find the perfect replacement. I've decided that systematic is the way to go. It's the wave of the future for serious shoppers, Screech. So I went to the library and looked in the Manhattan yellow pages. I'm doing it alphabetically. Barneys, Bendel, Bergdorf, Bloomingdale's . . ."

The eye in front of them disappeared. Obviously, Nanny was not interested in Lisa's shopping itinerary. The fact that Lisa Turtle was looking forward to shopping wouldn't be news at Bayside High.

From across the aisle, their other best friend, Jessie Spano, leaned over. Her hazel eyes were shining with excitement. "Lisa, you have plenty of time to organize your shopping," she said. "Look out the window! It's a gorgeous view. You can see Central Park!"

"Look!" A. C. Slater said. He pointed toward the window with his muscular arm, nearly smashing Jessie's nose.

Jessie pushed it aside. "And I bet that's the Museum of Natural History," she said, looking at a map and then looking down again. She gave Slater a deadpan look. "You might want to visit. That's where all your cavemen relatives live."

Lisa and Screech exchanged an amused glance. Jessie and Slater were an on-again, off-again couple, and right now they were definitely off. They were total opposites who never stopped arguing. Slater was a jock. He was captain of the wrestling team and quarterback on the football team. Jessie thought that both sports were examples of macho idiots trying to smash each other to smithereens. She was interested in art, politics, and the environment. Slater was interested in horror movies, junk food, and teasing Jessie unmercifully.

"Well," Lisa said in a low voice, "I know one thing. If the cable goes out in the hotel, at least we can rely on Jessie and Slater for entertainment."

In another minute, they were over the airport runway. The plane touched down, and the class burst into applause. They were finally in New York!

Chapter 2

▲ ▽ ▲ ▽ ▲ ▽ ▲

Everyone could hardly contain their excitement as the bus crossed a bridge and Manhattan loomed in front of them. Mr. Loomis tried to keep them all quiet, but everybody couldn't help yelling out when they saw a landmark.

"Look, the Empire State Building!" Daisy Tyler cried, widening her baby blue eyes.

Binky Grayson rolled his eyes. "Try again, Daisy. That's the *Chrysler* Building."

"So sue me," Daisy sniffed. "You know I don't know anything about cars."

"I hope the hotel is okay," Jessie said in an undertone to Lisa as the bus rolled through the city streets. She twisted a long, light brown curl around her finger nervously. Jessie's father worked for a big hotel chain, and he had swung a special deal for the class trip.

"The price was almost *too* good," Jessie continued worriedly. "I've never heard of the Metro Hotel. Daddy said it was small and elegant, but he's all the way out in San Francisco. What if the place is a dump?"

"I'm sure it will be beautiful," Lisa assured her. "Jessie, your father runs the best hotel in San Francisco. He's not going to pick a dump."

Just then, the bus pulled up in front of a large gray building with steel doors. "Oh, no," Jessie wailed. "It looks like a prison!"

"Come on, Spano," Slater said, reaching down and hauling her to her feet. His deep dimples flashed and his soft brown eyes twinkled. "It's time to serve out your sentence."

Filled with dread, Jessie followed Slater to the cold steel doors of the hotel. He pushed them open ahead of her, and Jessie hesitated. Slater laughed and grabbed her arm, pulling her forward into the lobby. Jessie kept her eyes closed.

Then she heard the reaction of the kids around her. "Wow," someone breathed. "Cool," someone said. "Awesome," someone exclaimed.

Jessie opened her eyes. It was gorgeous! She was standing in a soaring atrium with a dramatic black-and-white marble floor. The long reception desk was light wood with copper inlays, and oversized couches covered in purple velvet looked inviting. Shops lined the atrium, selling everything from jewelry to Swiss chocolates. On a second level, Jessie could glimpse a cappuccino bar.

Slater gave a low whistle. "If this is a prison," he said, "sign me up for life!"

Mr. Loomis returned from the reception desk, where he'd been checking everyone in. He clapped his hands. "All right, everybody," he said. "I have the room assignments. Remember, we are *guests* at this hotel. That means we're on our best behavior at all times—and that includes you, Mr. Morris."

Zack sighed. Sometimes it was tough having his reputation. You got in trouble even *before* you did anything.

"Okay," Mr. Loomis continued, "let's all head for our rooms. Check your schedule—you'll see that we meet back down here in fifteen minutes."

"I saw the Hard Rock Cafe down the street," Zack offered. "Can we head there for a snack?"

Mr. Loomis shook his head. "Look at your handout, Mr. Morris. After the fifteen-minute check-in period, we're going for a tour of Carnegie Hall."

Everyone groaned.

"It's of great historical interest," Mr. Loomis said sternly. "Tchaikovsky was the guest conductor during opening week."

"And afterward, we can get huge corned beef sandwiches and sodas at the Carnegie Deli!" Ms. McCracken said, and everyone cheered. Mr. Loomis gave Ms. McCracken a sour look.

"Made for each other," Kelly murmured to Zack.

"Maybe I should move the bulldozer up to Tuesday's plan," Zack said with a sigh.

Zack headed up to his room with Slater and Screech. After he'd washed up, he went through the drawers of the desk and found Metro Hotel stationery. While Slater flipped through the cable channels and Screech noisily splashed water in the bathroom, Zack sat down at the desk.

He chewed on a pen for a moment and then wrote carefully:

> *Dear Maisie,*
> *I hope our differences won't prevent us from being friends. I admit I was a stuffy jerk at the meeting. Let's pretend it never happened. So don't mention this letter or my apology. We'll just start over. No RSVP necessary.*

Zack signed it Willard Loomis and slipped it into an envelope. Slater was still checking out the TV, so Zack told him he'd meet him down in the lobby. He'd already noted what room Maisie McCracken had gone into. On the way, he saw a room-service tray left outside someone's door. There was a rose in a bud vase, and he plucked the rose and left it with the letter outside Ms. McCracken's door.

The plan was in motion. Whistling, Zack headed for the elevator.

▲   ▼   ▲

Screech finished washing up and went downstairs to the lobby. Zack was talking to Kelly, so Screech headed outside. He had about five minutes before Mr. Loomis herded them out, and he wanted to get the feel of the city.

As soon as he pushed open the door, he was met with the noise of traffic and the sight of pedestrians swirling around him. The Bayside High track team had nothing on New Yorkers, Screech thought. Everyone looked like they were doing the fifty-yard dash.

The door behind him opened, and Screech saw Nanny Parker come out. Her face was flushed with excitement, and she gazed around inquisitively. The last thing Screech wanted to do was talk to Nanny, so he quickly moved a few feet farther down the sidewalk, pretending not to see her.

He was so busy pretending not to see Nanny that he nearly knocked over an older woman who was standing in the shadow of a building awning next door.

"Oops," Screech said, steadying her elbow. "I'm really sorry. I didn't see you."

The woman was a few inches shorter than he

was, and she squinted up at him. "You've got to be from out of town," she said. "No New Yorker would be so polite."

"I'm from California," Screech admitted. Now that he had a chance to look, he noticed that the woman was shabbily dressed in a loose pair of khaki pants and an old sweater. She also had on an old raincoat and sneakers. Her wispy gray hair was pulled back with an elastic band. She didn't have any makeup on, and her face was pale. Still, she had nice features, and her eyes were a nice shade of blue. Next to her was a big shopping bag filled with sweaters that looked even older than the one she was wearing. Screech wondered if she was homeless.

"I used to live in California," the woman said. "Enjoy your stay in New York, young man."

She moved off toward the door of the hotel. Screech watched her as she placed a hand on the ornate bronze door handles. The doorman was ushering a hotel guest into a cab and didn't see her. Screech wondered if she'd be able to manage the heavy door. He started to go forward to help, but the woman turned around and walked a few steps away. Then she stopped, turned, and headed for the door again.

The doorman turned from the cab and saw her. He walked toward her quickly, frowning. "Can I help you?" he asked.

"I just wanted—" the woman said in a low voice.

"Are you a guest in the hotel?" the doorman asked brusquely.

"No," the woman said. "But—"

"Well, you'd better move along, then," the doorman said. "We don't allow panhandlers around here."

The woman hesitated only a fraction of a second, then turned away.

"That's awful," Nanny Parker said. Screech turned and saw that she was standing next to him. "The doorman didn't have to be so mean."

"I'll say," Screech said. He hurried after the woman, Nanny at his heels. "Ma'am?" he called. "Can I help you?"

The woman turned slowly. "No," she said. "I'm afraid not. But thank you, young man."

She looked so skinny and forlorn that Screech dug into his jeans pocket and found the twenty-dollar bill he'd put there earlier. He held it out to her. She stared at it a moment with a faint smile.

"You're a good boy," she said to Screech. "I hope you have a good time in New York." She started to walk away, but Screech took a step and slipped the bill into the pocket of her baggy sweater. The woman didn't notice and just kept on walking away.

"That was really nice of you, Screech," Nanny said.

Screech blushed. Of all the people who had to

see that, Nanny Parker was the worst. "I hope I don't read about it in the *Bayside Banner*," he said, glowering at Nanny.

Nanny looked hurt for a minute, and Screech was surprised. He didn't know Nanny Parker could ever feel hurt. She didn't have enough heart. But then her face changed back into the airy, superior expression she usually wore.

"Don't worry," she said flippantly. "You're not newsworthy anymore, Screech. Ever since you broke up with *Crystal*, that is. That was such a short romance. Too bad nobody ever met her."

Uh-oh. It looked like Lisa hadn't covered up well enough. Nanny suspected the truth!

Screech was relieved when Mr. Loomis walked out of the hotel. "Powers! Parker!" he bellowed. "Get in here on the double! You're holding up the whole class."

Screech hurried behind Nanny. That had been a close one. But now he knew that Nanny was on his trail, trying to dig up dirt. He'd better work hard to stay out of her way!

▲   ▼   ▲

The tour of Carnegie Hall turned out to be pretty interesting, after all. Then Ms. McCracken led them to a deli where they had huge, overstuffed sandwiches and cole slaw. Afterward, they all were too full to do anything but take a short walk to Rockefeller Center. By then, everyone's feet were dragging, and Mr. Loomis suggested they go back and go to bed early.

"Get over your jet lag, gang," he said cheerfully. "Tomorrow morning, we hit Ellis Island. Lots of history there."

"And the Metropolitan Museum of Art in the afternoon," Ms. McCracken said. "Lots of *art* there." She gave Mr. Loomis a friendly smile, then winked at him.

Mr. Loomis looked surprised. Then he blushed. "Uh, let's get moving, troops," he said, taking off for the hotel at a fast clip.

Zack nudged Kelly. "Did you see that? My plan is working."

"I don't know about this," Kelly said worriedly. "Mr. Loomis is super strict. What if he finds out you forged that note? You could get into major trouble, Zack. He might even send you home."

"Mr. Loomis won't find out," Zack said. "I'm positive. And even if he *does*, he'd never be able to figure out it was me. And if he *did* figure out it was me, he'd be so in love, he'd be grateful to me for setting him up with Ms. McCracken."

Kelly sighed. "Maybe. But if you're wrong, it's going to be awfully hard to go steady with someone who'll be in detention for the rest of senior year."

Chapter 3

▲ ▼ ▲ ▼ ▲ ▼ ▲

The next morning, Zack dressed quickly and dashed out into the hall. He plucked a rose from a flower arrangement on the hall table and left it right outside Maisie McCracken's door. Then he quickly made for the elevator and went down to the lobby.

He was the first one down, so he prowled around the lobby, window-shopping. He wished he had money to buy Kelly a pair of diamond earrings or even the silver necklace he saw in one store window. But Kelly didn't care about expensive gifts. She was the best girlfriend in the world. And if only he could get Mr. Loomis off their backs, they could get in some serious romance time.

Zack saw the elevator doors open, and Mr. Loomis got out. A second later, another elevator opened and Ms. McCracken got off. They both seemed awkward as they greeted each other, so Zack decided to amble over to help things along.

"Isn't this a great lobby?" he asked as he came up.

"Fantastic," Mr. Loomis said quickly.

"Fabulous," Ms. McCracken said in a too-bright voice.

Obviously, they were grateful to have someone else to talk to. "Even if I never left the lobby, I'd feel like I saw New York," Zack said.

Ms. McCracken laughed. "I don't know about that," she said. "But at least you'd be well fed. They have four different restaurants here."

"I want to try the cappuccino bar," Zack said.

"Actually, what I'm dying to do is hit the pool on the roof," Ms. McCracken admitted.

"I'm with Zack," Mr. Loomis said. "I'll stick with the food. After the cappuccino, I'd head right over there to Le Chocolaterie. They have the very best chocolate in the whole world."

Just then, Lisa joined them. "What I'm dying to do is hit that boutique over there with my father's credit card," she confessed. "Unfortunately," she added with a grin, "he didn't give it to me. He knows better."

Ms. McCracken suddenly reached over to Lisa's purse. "Lisa, watch out!" she exclaimed. "Your purse is hanging open."

Lisa snapped it shut. "Not again," she moaned. "I've just *got* to get a new purse—and soon."

"Be very careful," Ms. McCracken warned. "We're taking the subway this morning."

"I'll keep my eye on it," Lisa promised.

While Lisa told Ms. McCracken about her alphabetical shopping plans, Zack slipped away and nonchalantly crossed the lobby. After he glanced back to make sure that no one was looking, he quickly ducked into Le Chocolaterie.

"Can I help you?" a woman asked in a French accent.

"I'd like a box of assorted chocolates," Zack said.

"Would you like the fifty-dollar size or the seventy-five-dollar size?" the woman asked.

Zack gulped. "I didn't say I wanted them gold plated," he blurted.

The woman raised an eyebrow. "Perhaps, for you, the twenty-five-dollar box." She held up a tiny, gold-foil box with a pink ribbon. "Yes?"

Twenty-five dollars was a lot of money for a matchbox-size box of chocolates. But if it meant he'd get one free afternoon, it was worth it. "All right," Zack said. He handed over the money. "Can you send them to Room twelve sixteen?"

"Would you like a card?"

Zack nodded, and she handed over a small white card. *Remember, no thank yous!* he scribbled on it. He handed the card to the woman, then peeked outside. Mr. Loomis was checking the class list, so he quickly dashed out and went around the other side of the group. He took his place beside Kelly.

"Where have you been?" Kelly asked under her breath.

"Buying a bulldozer," Zack muttered.

"Okay, we're all here," Mr. Loomis said. "On to Ellis Island!"

▲   ▼   ▲

On the boat over to Ellis Island, Nanny kept her nose buried in a stack of newspapers. Screech was glad she wasn't following him around the boat, sniffing after any news he might let slip about the imaginary Crystal Spalding.

Mr. Loomis stayed in the stern, talking to studious Alan Zobel, and Ms. McCracken stood right in the bow, her scarf flapping wildly, while she joked with a few members of the Art Club.

"So much for your plan," Kelly told Zack as they stood by the rail, watching the Statue of Liberty loom closer and closer. "They couldn't be farther apart."

"I haven't given up yet," Zack said. "Just wait and see."

The tour of Ellis Island turned out to be fascinating, even though Mr. Loomis had recommended it.

The gang was interested in the artifacts the immigrants had left behind, and listened wide-eyed to the guard as she described the medical procedures they had to go through before being allowed into the country.

"Wow," Kelly said, as they walked out of the Great Hall into the fresh morning air. "I never realized how much courage my ancestors had."

"Wait a second, Kelly," Jessie said. "I thought your family had been in California for generations."

Kelly nodded. "My father's family, yes. But my mother's family is from Scotland. I researched them for my paper on genealogy last fall. I had to trace how my mother's ancestors arrived in this country. My great-grandfather came from a family with six brothers, and three of them emigrated to the U.S. My great-grandfather landed in Philadelphia and went straight out West. He already had a job in California. But I found out that his older brother came over earlier, in eighteen seventy, and settled in New York."

"Do you know that part of the family?" Jessie asked curiously.

Kelly shook her head. "Not at all. I don't even know if they're still here. You see, my great-grandfather and his brother weren't close, and they lost touch. They came from a family of ten children, and my great-grandfather's older brother was about twenty years older than he was." Kelly grinned. "Big families run in my family, obviously." Kelly came from a fun-loving, boisterous family of six kids.

"Hey," Jessie said, "let's look on the wall and see if we can find his name."

There was a long wall on the island where the family names of immigrants were engraved. Many families had contributed to the Ellis Island foundation to inscribe their ancestors' names on the wall.

"That's a great idea," Kelly said. "I remember my great-grandfather's name was Lenihan."

The gang hurried over to the *L*'s and began to search for the name. Zack found it. "Look, Kelly!" he cried. "Here it is!"

"Wow," Kelly said. "I know this might not be *my* Lenihan, but I bet my mom would be thrilled, anyway. I have to tell her I saw the Lenihan name."

"Did you say Lenihan?" Nanny Parker asked, looking up from the bench where she was still reading the morning papers.

Kelly nodded. "It's a family name."

"There's no scoop here, Nanny," Screech said. "This story is over a hundred years old."

Nanny ignored Screech. "There's a really famous socialite in New York named Marion Lenihan," she said. "I've been reading about her in all the gossip columns."

"Really?" Kelly asked. "What do they say about her?"

Nanny reached for another paper. "Well, my favorite columnist, Billy Cahill, says that Marion is the heiress to the James MacPherson Lenihan steel fortune."

"Was your ancestor's name James?" Zack asked Kelly excitedly.

She shook her head. "I think it was Andrew," she said.

"Too bad," Slater said. "If you were an heiress, I was going to suggest that you buy lunch today."

Nanny picked up another paper. "And *this* one says that Marion has the most famous jewel collection in New York, including the ruby earrings formerly worn by some Indian princess. And she's a strict vegetarian. And *this* one says that she's donating her famous art collection to the Metropolitan Museum. They're having a cocktail party there this evening to honor her."

"Hey," Zack said. "That's where *we're* headed this afternoon. What if we bump into her?"

"I'd say 'Excuse me' and keep walking," Kelly said with a laugh. "I'm sure I'm not related to Marion Lenihan."

"You never know, Kelly," Nanny Parker said. "I mean, it could have been another one of the brothers. The Lenihans made their fortune in the eighteen eighties."

"It's silly," Kelly protested. "I'm sure my mother would know if her side of the family had money. Believe me, she could have used it. She worked three jobs to get through college."

"Oh, well," Slater said. "It was nice while it lasted."

Jessie looked at the dock and saw the ferry approaching. "It's time to go back. I wonder why Mr. Loomis hasn't lined us all up in single file?"

"That's why," Slater said with a grin.

He pointed to a bench in a nook overlooking the sea. Mr. Loomis and Ms. McCracken were sitting together, involved in what seemed to be an intense conversation.

"Looks like your plan is working, Zack," Kelly whispered. When Zack didn't respond, she poked him. "Zack?"

"Huh?" Slowly, Zack came out of the dreamworld he'd entered when he'd heard the words *fortune* and *heiress*.

He looked over at the bench. "Oh, Mr. Loomis and Ms. McCracken. Far out," he said distractedly. "We'd better get to the ferry."

Kelly gave him a curious look, but Zack had already zapped back into fantasyland. Of course he loved Kelly for herself. But since he already *did*, it wouldn't hurt to have a couple of million dollars to boot. He pictured himself and Kelly jetting from Switzerland to Paris to New York, staying in fabulous hotels. The Alps in winter, the Bahamas in summer. Or was it the other way around? Whatever—he would figure it out.

Then Zack got a brainstorm.

"Time out, gang," he said. "I've got an idea."

"Uh-oh," Kelly moaned.

"Why don't we crash Marion Lenihan's party?" Zack asked. "Then Kelly could meet her and tell her who she is. We could find out once and for all if Kelly is related to the famous Lenihans."

"Dream on, preppy," Slater chortled.

Zack shrugged. "And if she's not, we can still scarf up lots of hors d'oeuvres."

"Count me in," Slater said promptly.

"I don't know, Zack," Jessie said. "Those fancy cocktail parties have lots of security."

"I have yet to meet a security guard I can't bamboozle," Zack said. "Look, we can get dressed up when we go back to the hotel for our scheduled wash-up time. That way, we'll at least look like the other guests."

Screech frowned. "I don't know about this," he said. "I don't want to get in trouble with Mr. Loomis. He's my favorite teacher. And he's going to give a special lecture on the Etruscan collection. I wouldn't want to miss it."

"We *would* have to get dressed up," Lisa said slowly. "And I *did* bring my pink taffeta dress. . . ."

"Zack, this is crazy!" Kelly protested. Then she

weakened. "But I *would* like to find out if I'm related to her."

"Let's do it," Slater said. "Crashing parties is my second favorite sport."

"What's your favorite sport?" Jessie asked. "Football or wrestling? Or should I say crashing your helmet into someone's face or strangling them until they turn purple?"

"It's wrestling," Slater said. His deep dimples flashed, and he slipped his muscular arms around Jessie's waist. "Don't you remember my holds, momma?"

"Not if I can help it," Jessie said, wiggling out of his arms. But there was a pink blush on her cheeks, and she didn't seem to mind Slater's comment too much.

"Then you're with me?" Zack asked the gang.

Everyone nodded. "We're with you, preppy," Slater said. "Just don't get us arrested."

"It'll be a piece of cake," Zack said.

"They'll have dessert, too?" Screech asked. His frizzy curls shook as he nodded happily. "Then count me in!"

Chapter 4

▲　▼　▲　▼　▲　▼　▲

After lunch at an old tavern in lower Manhattan, Mr. Loomis led them on a re-creation of the route Washington took on the very first presidential inauguration day. Then they walked around in a cemetery near Trinity Church, and Mr. Loomis put flowers on Alexander Hamilton's grave. Finally, they took the subway back up to the hotel for Mr. Loomis's planned "fifteen-minute—and I don't mean sixteen-minute—pit stop" before heading to the Metropolitan.

Most of the kids stayed down in the lobby to browse or to grab one of the delicious pastries at the cappuccino bar, but Zack and the gang raced upstairs to change. They'd never get into a fancy party wearing jeans.

When Zack came out of his room, he saw Kelly

leaving hers. He whistled in appreciation. Kelly was wearing a new dress that was the dark blue of the evening sky. It matched her eyes perfectly. Her long, dark hair was pinned up in a French twist and sparkly earrings in the shape of stars were in her ears.

"Wow," Zack said. "You *do* look like an heiress."

Kelly smiled. "You look great, too, Zack."

"Maybe Marion will believe us when we tell her that you might be related," Zack said, glancing in the mirror and smoothing back his blond hair. "If not," he said cheerfully, "maybe she'll adopt us."

Jessie and Lisa came out of the room next. Lisa was frowning. "I can't believe it," she said in distress. "I forgot to bring the purse that matched this dress."

"Oh, my gosh," Zack cried theatrically. "What a disaster!"

"You don't understand, Zack," Lisa said. "I have to take my *everyday* purse." She held up her pink purse despairingly.

"It matches your dress," Zack said.

"But it has a white clasp, and I'm wearing black shoes!" Lisa wailed.

"That does it, Lisa," Zack said flatly. "We'll have to catch the next flight back to Palisades."

Lisa rolled her eyes. "Men!" she cried dramatically.

"You rang?" Screech asked, hurtling out of his

hotel room. He was dressed in his best plaid jacket and a matching cummerbund.

"I didn't say *dweebs*, I said *men*," Lisa said.

Slater ambled toward them with his easygoing stride. But he stopped dead when he saw Jessie. Her long, curly hair was held up by a rhinestone clip, and it tumbled down to her bare left shoulder. Her form-fitting emerald green dress showed off her long, shapely legs. He recovered quickly and joined them. it would be death to let Jessie know that he was still attracted to her.

"We'd better ring for the elevator," Zack said. "Slater, push the button."

Slater couldn't help it; he couldn't stop staring at Jessie. How could he ever have let her go?

Zack nudged him. "Slater!"

"Right." Slater hit the UP button.

Zack blew out a sigh of exasperation, reached past Slater, and pushed the DOWN button. "You need to get your eyes examined," he said.

"You're not kidding, preppy," Slater said, still checking out Jessie. *Maybe that was the reason he let her go—bad eyesight.*

Jessie stared at the elevator indicator. She had noticed Slater staring at her, and she could feel her neck turning red. She and Slater had decided to be just friends. Why was he staring at her in that very *un*-friendly way? It was a very *boyfriend* way. There was no way she'd *ever* go back to that curly headed Neanderthal. No matter how cute he was!

When the gang got off in the lobby, the entire Bayside group swiveled and stared. The girls smoothed their pretty dresses self-consciously, and Slater nervously pulled at his tie.

"I didn't know this was a *formal* tour," Greg Tolan said, and his buddy Jeremy Frears guffawed.

"It's important to always look one's best," Zack said airily. "Right, Mr. Loomis?"

Mr. Loomis didn't seem to hear him. Zack saw that he was off in a corner, offering Ms. McCracken a chocolate from a tiny gold-foil box. Zack drifted closer. Mr. Loomis had a completely goony expression on his face as Ms. McCracken popped a chocolate into her mouth. Zack sighed as six dollars of his hard-earned money from cutting lawns slid down the art teacher's throat. But it was worth it when he saw the smile Ms. McCracken bestowed on Mr. Loomis.

"Delicious," Ms. McCracken said. "I can't believe you have an anonymous admirer. Maybe one of the girls has a crush on you."

"Maybe," Mr. Loomis said, sounding as though he was playing along. "Too bad I can't thank whoever it was. But if I *could* thank the person, I would say that it's the nicest thing anyone's ever done for me."

"This little box of candy?" Ms. McCracken's green eyes twinkled. "Maybe you should get out more."

"I plan to," Mr. Loomis said meaningfully.

"Well," Ms. McCracken said, checking her watch, "we'd better go. I want to get from the Middle Ages to Picasso before the museum closes."

Mr. Loomis was staring dreamily at Ms. McCracken. "Right."

"So let's go," Ms. McCracken said.

"Right," Mr. Loomis said tenderly. "Where?"

"To the museum," Ms. McCracken repeated.

"Right."

"Willard?"

"Yes, Maisie?"

Zack closed his eyes in bliss. They were on a first-name basis! It must have been the chocolate.

Ms. McCracken giggled. She gave Mr. Loomis a little push. "Let's herd 'em up and move 'em out."

Mr. Loomis gave her a last adoring gaze, then clapped his hands and told everyone it was time to get moving.

Zack trailed out of the hotel and headed to the Madison Avenue bus with the others. He hoped his good luck was holding. Crashing a society bash would be a lot harder to accomplish than the Loomis-McCracken merger. He was sure of it!

▲   ▼   ▲

"This is a Claude Monet," Ms. McCracken said. "It was painted in 1891. Later in the week when we visit the Museum of Modern Art, we can see his wonderful paintings of water lilies. Note the use of light and color."

Zack checked his watch. The cocktail party started at five, and it was five-fifteen. The class had been through the Middle Ages, the Renaissance, and some other period that was a blur of portraits. Now they were only halfway through the Impressionists. Zack and the gang could sneak away and be back before Ms. McCracken had made it to the twentieth century.

He tugged on Kelly's arm, and she nodded. She poked Jessie, who poked Slater, who poked Lisa, who poked Screech.

"Ow!" Screech said, rubbing his arm.

"Shhh," Zack said. "It's the signal."

"No, it's Seurat," Screech said in a loud whisper, naming the painter Ms. McCracken was now explaining.

Lisa rolled her eyes and then clapped her hand over Screech's mouth. "I'll take care of him," she murmured to Zack.

Zack nodded. Ms. McCracken was totally wrapped up in the paintings. Mr. Loomis was totally wrapped up in Ms. McCracken. This would be a cinch. As the class moved into the next gallery, the gang beat a hasty retreat.

Zack had already checked out the museum floor plan, so he led them through Islamic vases and

Egyptian mummies until they got to the wing that housed the Temple of Dendur. They started toward the doors, but a guard materialized and stood in front of them.

"Sorry," he said. "This section is closed for a private function."

Zack moved forward, smiling his most charming smile. He thought of Skippy Tolliver, who wore a blue blazer with a crest on the pocket even in gym class, and borrowed his lockjaw accent. "We're here for Mrs. Lenihan's party," he said. "Auntie Marion is going to be *furious* that we're so late."

"*Is* she," the guard said. He crossed his arms and didn't move.

"I call her auntie, but she's actually my third cousin once removed on Mummy's side," Zack explained. He held up his fingers and clicked off names one by one. "You see, Mummy's sister Mimi married Duffy Corchran, whose sister was Missy Mufferson, who as you know made a pos-i-tive-ly *brilliant* marriage to Dinky Duncan, whose aunt was Muffy Lenihan, so you see how close we all are."

"I'm sure Missy, Muffy, and Mimi will be crushed not to see you," the guard said.

"Not to mention Mummy," Zack said with a winning smile.

"Did Mummy, Mimi, Muffy, or Missy happen to give you an invitation?" the guard asked.

"Well, of course, why didn't you say so?" Zack patted his pockets. "Oh, dear. Oh, no."

"Don't tell me," the guard said. "You forgot it."

"I *was* going to wear the gray cashmere," Zack said with a sigh. He turned to Kelly. "You made me change into the navy."

"Oooo, sorry," Kelly said. "Remember, you spilled champagne on the gray?"

"I'm so clumsy," Zack said confidentially to the guard. "That's what Mummy always said. Oh, dear, Kelly. Now you'll miss seeing Auntie Marion."

"I'll tell her you stopped by," the guard said. "Now beat it."

What could they do? Zack turned away. That routine had always worked for the Palisades Country Club formals. Who knew that New York City security guards would be so tough?

Suddenly Screech spoke up. "As long as we're leaving, let's stop by and see the Etruscan collection."

The gang exchanged glances. What was Screech up to?

"Yes," Zack said, playing along. "Mummy just donated some pottery shards."

"Could you tell me how to get there?" Screech asked the guard.

The guard sighed heavily. "Sure. Just go back the way you came but make a left. Go through Arms and Armor and make a left at the medieval horse armor. Then take your next right at the Chinese Ming vases, go directly through the Islamic art section, and make a left at the rugs."

"Okay," Screech said. "A right at Arms and Armor—"

"No, go *through* Armor."

"Right."

"No, *left*. After the horse armor."

"Right. I mean left. And then follow the rugs—" Screech pointed down the hall.

"No, first you have to hit the Ming vases."

"Hit the Ming vases?" Screech asked, shocked. "But aren't they really delicate?"

Zack exchanged a look with Kelly. The guard was so engrossed with giving Screech directions that he was moving away from the doors, pointing the way each time Screech messed up. Jessie and Slater exchanged a knowing look with Zack, then moved forward to stand between the guard and Zack and Kelly.

"What about the Hellenistic period?" Jessie asked. "Do we make a left there?"

As the frustrated guard tried to explain all over again, Zack grabbed Kelly's hand and pulled her through the doors. Lisa just managed to slip in behind them.

"I didn't wear my best dress for nothing," she murmured happily, smoothing the skirt.

The three of them took a deep breath and gazed at the scene before them, openmouthed. The first thing they noticed was the Temple of Dendur, a huge stone structure in the middle of the atrium.

"Wow," Kelly said. "I feel like I'm in Egypt."

"I read that it dates from 10 B.C.," Zack said. "Can you imagine that? It used to stand on the banks of the Nile. It's really impressive."

"I'll say," Lisa said. "I think it's a real Valentino."

"Huh?" Zack said. He looked at Lisa, and she was staring at a woman's dress.

"Well," she said defensively when she noticed Zack looking at her, "who wants to look at a musty old temple when there're couture dresses around?"

People swirled around them, dressed in elegant suits and gorgeous cocktail dresses. Everywhere they turned, they were dazzled by the jewels around women's necks and the beautiful clothes. The huge hall where they were standing had one whole wall made of glass. Through it, they could see the lush lawns and trees of Central Park. Long tables had been set up in front of the glass wall, and white-jacketed waiters were busily setting up a buffet. Other waiters circulated throughout the room with tiny hors d'oeuvres and glasses of champagne.

"Pinch me," Lisa breathed. "I must be dreaming, or this is heaven on earth. Look at the jewels!"

"Look at the food," Zack said.

"Look at the security guards," Kelly said.

"We'd better find Marion before we get caught," Zack said. He scanned the room, looking for her. Marion Lenihan should be easy to spot. He had memorized her face from the society page, and he knew she was almost six feet tall.

Just then, Zack caught sight of Marion. She was standing directly in front of the temple. She almost looked like a high priestess in her scarlet gown with the gold sash. Even from here, Zack was practically blinded by the diamond necklace she wore. Large rubies winked in her ears. He couldn't wait to start calling her Auntie Marion for real.

"There she is," Zack said in a low voice. "Come on."

Kelly started forward, but her feet began to drag. "I can't," she said. "Just look at her! She'll eat me alive."

"We'll be right with you," Lisa said soothingly.

"We've made it this far," Zack said. "Kelly, you've got to follow through."

Reluctantly, Kelly headed for Marion. She waited until the man Marion was talking to was hailed by someone across the room. Then she quickly walked up to her, Lisa and Zack by her side.

"Mrs. Lenihan?" Kelly held out her hand. "Hi, I'm Kelly Kapowski."

Marion took her hand and shook it. "Zapowski? I don't think we've met."

"Kapowski. And, no, we haven't met. I'm from California," Kelly said.

"Oh. Bel Air?"

Kelly shook her head.

"Palm Springs?"

Kelly shook her head and grinned. "Palisades. It's a little town south of L.A."

Marion sniffed. "I see. Is there some *reason* I should know you?"

"Not really," Kelly said.

"Because I went over the guest list myself," Marion said haughtily. "And I don't remember a Zoowowski."

"Kapowski," Kelly said.

Marion frowned. "Did you come with some-one else?"

"Sure," Kelly said. "I came with Zack." She pushed Zack forward. "And Lisa." She reached be-hind her and yanked Lisa closer. She was starting to get nervous, and she needed some moral support.

"And which of *you* was invited?" Marion asked. Her bright blue eyes were inspecting them beadily.

Zack saw it was time for some serious scamming. "We have a friend in common," he said. "Muffy wanted us to say hello." Every socialite knew a Muffy, he figured.

"Muffy who?" Marion asked suspiciously.

"Muffy from Palm Beach," Zack went on. "You know Muffy. Going here, going there, even in the off-season. She's such a scream."

"Oh, you mean Muffy Andover," Marion said.

"Exactly," Zack said, relieved. "Good old Muffy."

"Good old Muffy," Marion said. "Such a shame, her dying last year."

Zack swallowed. "I hadn't heard. No wonder she hasn't called me. What a tragic thing. Taken so young."

"She was ninety-seven," Marion said.

"But so young at heart!" Zack said quickly.

"Zack," Kelly said, "this isn't working. Maybe I should explain. . . ."

"No need," Marion Lenihan said frostily. "I know a gate crasher when I see one." She whipped her head back and forth, her ruby earrings swinging as she angrily searched the crowd. "And as soon as I can find a guard, I'll have you thrown out!"

Out of the corner of his eye, Zack saw the security guard Screech had bamboozled enter the party. Marion signaled him. *Uh-oh*, Zack thought. *This party is definitely over!*

"Sorry, Marion," he said. "We simply *must* run. Give my regards to Muffy!"

Chapter 5

▲ ▼ ▲ ▼ ▲ ▼ ▲

Zack pulled Kelly and Lisa through the crowd, but he blundered into a group of people who were heading toward the buffet table. They were politely pushing their way toward the lobster mousse, and Zack lost his grip on Kelly's hand. Then he lost Lisa. Zack was carried along in the crowd and found himself smashed against the wall as they surged by. When he was finally able to look around, Kelly and Lisa were nowhere in sight.

Zack saw the security guard searching the crowd. Any minute now, he'd be over in this area. Frantically, Zack looked for the nearest exit. He'd have to cross the entire length of the room to get there, and the guard was getting closer and closer!

On a small chair behind the buffet table, Zack spied a chef's hat and one of the white coats worn by the food servers. Quickly, he snatched the coat and slipped it on, then put the chef's hat on his head. He turned away and pretended to fuss with a bunch of weird lettuce.

"That's in case we run out," a voice said behind him. It was low and husky, but friendly, too. But would it be friendly when Zack turned around and was unmasked?

"Oh," he said into the lettuce.

"They wanted frisee, but we couldn't get enough, so we got escarole, too," the voice continued. "Hopefully, we won't need to use it. Mrs. Lenihan could probably tell the difference. She's a strict vegetarian. Not to mention a fussy snob." An adorable giggle followed.

"Mmmff," Zack said.

"Hey, can you help me with this for a second?"

Zack sighed. The jig was up. He turned around slowly and looked into a pair of friendly amber eyes. They were long lashed and slightly tilted at the corners, and when the girl smiled, her eyes crinkled in the cutest way. She was holding a big tub full of salad greens, and she pointed to a large bowl with her chin. "If you could just hold this while I scoop out some more salad," she said.

"Right," Zack said. Obviously, the girl thought he worked there. Since there were so many waiters, they probably didn't all know each other.

The girl bent over to grab the greens with a large

set of tongs. Her fuzzy blond curls brushed against Zack's cheek as she tossed the greens from the tub into the bowl.

"Thanks," she said, straightening up. "I'm Alex Washburne, by the way. You must be the special chef they hired for tonight."

"Right," Zack said.

"I tasted the lobster corn cakes you made," Alex said. "They were really exceptional."

"Thank you," Zack said.

"I thought the addition of cilantro was inspired," Alex went on. She grinned. "As you might have guessed, I'm a chef, too. I went to the Culinary Academy, and I'm a sous-chef at a private club. That's how I got this gig. Mrs. Lenihan is on the board at the club, so some of the kitchen staff signed on for tonight. We cook for her all the time— phew! It isn't easy." Alex rolled her amber eyes.

Zack grinned. Alex Washburne had a way about her that he liked. She was so blunt and funny. A real New Yorker, he supposed. There was no softness in her manner, but he didn't miss it. He liked her snappy delivery and her way of grinning as though she were letting him in on a secret. "So where did you study?" Alex asked him as she expertly arranged a display of cold vegetables on a platter. "It's neat to see someone so young make it. Gives me hope."

"I studied in, uh, Paris," Zack improvised. "And

then I worked all over in California."

"So you got classical training and then got to experience all that innovation out there," Alex said, nodding. "The last time I went to L.A., all I did was eat. I love California cuisine."

"Me, too," Zack said. *Yeah, like pizza and burgers.*

"I like the Mexican influence," Alex said.

"I agree," Zack said. *As a matter of fact, Taco Delight is my favorite restaurant.*

"I noticed," Alex said, "those lobster corn cakes were really spicy." She drizzled a creamy sauce over the vegetables. "So do you live in New York now?"

"No, I'm just here to do a couple of special parties," Zack said. "But I'm thinking of moving here."

"Great! It's a fabulous city. And there's so many opportunities for talented chefs here. Of course," she admitted, "I haven't found them yet. But I keep knocking on doors." Alex smiled at him.

Zack thought she had just about the prettiest smile he'd ever seen. *Except for Kelly's, of course,* he amended quickly. Alex would be a fun person to date. All that energy and ambition must be exciting to be around.

"Maybe you could stop by the club while you're here," Alex said. "The chef there does some interesting things."

Zack looked over Alex's head and saw the security guard heading down the buffet table with an empty plate. Any minute now, he'd be reaching for the salad.

"I'll be really busy while I'm here," Zack said quickly.

"Oh, sure. I understand."

"And speaking of busy, I have another party to supervise," Zack babbled. "I've got to go. Nice meeting you, Alex." He took off, whipping off his chef's hat as he went.

Now that he was wearing the white coat, everyone looked right through him, thinking he was a waiter. Zack reached the exit easily. He pushed through the doors and unbuttoned the jacket as he ran down the hall. He stuffed it into a big Grecian urn as he ran past.

There was no telling where the Bayside group would be now. What if they'd gone back to the hotel? Mr. Loomis would kill him. Kelly was right— he might even send Zack home. He wasn't *that* much in love with Ms. McCracken yet.

Zack raced out into the lobby. He looked at the museum floor plan. This place was the biggest museum he'd ever seen. How would he ever find them? Would they be in the American Wing? Decorative Arts? Period Rooms? Post–Civil War Realism or Visionary Painting? Zack sighed in frustration.

Just then, he heard Daisy Tyler's high-pitched giggle. He looked across the lobby. Of course—

they were in the most important room of all. The gift shop!

Zack drifted into the gift shop and made his way casually over to where Lisa was examining T-shirts and tote bags and showing them to Kelly.

"Zack!" Kelly said. "Where have you been? I've been so worried. We're heading back to the hotel any minute, and I was going to tell Ms. McCracken that I couldn't find you. I was afraid that horrible guard had caught you."

Zack shook his head. "Almost, but not quite."

"Well, I'm glad you're finally here," Lisa said. Her arms were full of T-shirts and postcards and jewelry. "Now I can *really* concentrate on shopping."

"Lisa, you'd better close your purse," Kelly said. "They're going to think you're shoplifting."

Lisa snapped her purse shut. "Thanks, Kelly. Now come with me to the mirror. I want you to tell me which earrings to buy."

Kelly squeezed Zack's hand. "I'll be right back," she whispered.

Zack watched her go. He felt totally guilty about worrying Kelly. So totally guilty, in fact, that he had a feeling it wasn't just because he'd disappeared. It was because of how much he'd liked Alex Washburne's smile.

He'd never see Alex Washburne again, Zack told himself. That would definitely make his life easier.

But why was he just a little bit disappointed at the thought of it?

▲   ▼   ▲

The next morning, Kelly, Lisa, and Jessie woke early. Light peeked through the thick draperies at the window. Kelly got up and crossed to open them, and sunlight flooded the room.

"It's already Wednesday," Jessie said with a yawn. "The trip will be over before we know it. And I'm having so much fun."

"I can't believe Mr. Loomis let Ms. McCracken talk him into canceling the trip to Teddy Roosevelt's birthplace today," Lisa said. "I'm glad, though. I'd much rather go roller skating in Central Park. Even though Mr. Loomis is calling it an 'exercise segment,' it still sounds like fun."

Kelly grinned as she knotted the sash on her robe. "Think about it, you guys," she said. "We didn't get caught sneaking into that party last night. Zack's plan to get Mr. Loomis off our backs is working. I think the impossible just might happen—we might have a normal class trip. No disasters, just fun."

"Now, *that* will be unusual," Jessie said with a laugh. "Remember on our sophomore ski trip when Screech broke his leg?"

"After he smashed into a tree," Lisa said, giggling. "And on our San Francisco trip when Kelly got kidnapped?"

"Well, keep your fingers crossed," Kelly said with a giggle. "We still have plenty of days to go."

Just then, there was a banging on their door. The girls exchanged alarmed glances.

"Who is it?" Jessie called through the door.

"It's us!" Zack called. "Can we come in? We've got news!"

Jessie checked to make sure everyone was up and in their robes, then opened the door. The boys rushed in, each of them holding a newspaper.

"You're not going to believe this," Zack said, tossing the newspaper on the bed. "Look!"

Lisa gasped as she examined the picture on the front page. "That's Marion Lenihan! 'Jewel Heist at the Met,' " Lisa read aloud from the paper. She looked up. "What does this mean?"

"Check this out," Slater said. He tossed his paper down beside Zack's. The headline read: NOT FAIR-O: MYSTERIOUS TEMPLE HEIST.

Jessie was rapidly scanning the article. "One of Mrs. Lenihan's priceless ruby earrings was stolen last night."

"Wow," Kelly breathed. "Just think. We were at a party with a jewel thief!"

"Poor Mrs. Lenihan," Lisa said.

"She's probably insured," Slater said.

"No, I meant this picture is just awful," Lisa said, squinting at the paper. "I'd be absolutely mortified."

"There's more," Zack said grimly.

"Do they have any suspects?" Kelly asked.

"You might say so," Slater said.

Jessie looked up from the paper. "They have a pretty good idea who did it," she said slowly.

"Oh, good," Kelly said. "I hope they catch them."

"Me, too," Lisa agreed. "Those ruby earrings were *gorgeous*. I wonder why they didn't take both of them. Gosh, who do they think it was? Some romantic French gang who operates on the Riviera?"

Zack shook his head. "Not exactly."

"It's a gang a little closer to home," Jessie said. She read from the paper. "A trio of gate crashers are suspected. Two young women diverted Mrs. Lenihan's attention while a man slipped the ruby from her. The unusually young gang of jewel thieves then vanished in the crowd. 'I suspected them right away,' Mrs. Lenihan reported in a shaky voice. 'They looked completely out of place, and their clothes were all wrong. They looked very shifty to me.' "

Kelly gasped. "We're the suspects!"

"I'm afraid so," Zack said.

"But how could they think that we did the

heist?" Kelly demanded. "I can't even *spell* it."

"I hope this doesn't mean that Auntie Marion will disinherit Kelly," Screech said.

"It says that the thieves are thought to have three more cohorts who were foiled by a guard. I guess that's me, Slater, and Screech," Jessie murmured, still reading. "They have pretty accurate descriptions of Zack, Lisa, and Kelly."

"Accurate?" Lisa squeaked. "Marion said my clothes were all wrong. How could my dress be wrong? It's taffeta!" She sank down on the chair. "This is the worst thing that ever happened to me. Accused of being a jewel thief *and* having no fashion sense all in the same night!"

"No sweat, Lisa," Slater said soothingly. "I just thought of some good news."

Lisa looked up at him with unhappy brown eyes. "What?" she sniffed.

Slater grinned. "Where you're going, I don't think you'll have to worry about clothes."

Chapter 6

▲ ▼ ▲ ▼ ▲ ▼ ▲

Somehow, the gang had to pull themselves together and act normal. But for Zack, acting normal on a roller-skating rink wasn't easy even under the best circumstances. Skating was not his best sport.

After he'd bruised his knees and skinned his left elbow, Zack decided to call it quits. He crashed against a side railing and leaned against it to watch. Every so often, one of the girls would skate by and ask him if he'd thought of a way to get them out of the mess they were in. Then Screech would crash into the railing next to him and tell him that he was sure Zack would come up with a brainstorm.

Zack practiced frowning as though he was cooking up some incredible plan. But what the gang didn't know was that his mind was completely blank. This just might be more trouble than he could handle. Should they simply walk into a police station and tell them that they were searching for a group of beach-loving Californians who wouldn't even steal a minute of your time, let alone a jewel? Or should they just lay low and hope no cop recognized them?

Zack couldn't even get any enjoyment out of watching Ms. McCracken try to teach the awkward Willard Loomis how to skate. He'd done it this time. He'd really gotten his friends into hot water. He watched them approach worriedly.

"So?" Kelly asked, adjusting her scarf. "What's the plan?"

"What did you come up with, Zack?" Lisa asked. "Our pictures are probably on the wall of the post office right now."

Just then, Mr. Loomis gave the ear-splitting whistle that told them the "exercise segment" was over. Everyone went over to return their skates and put their shoes back on. That gave Zack a few extra minutes to continue to *not* come up with a brilliant plan.

Mr. Loomis whistled again. He gave a quick grin to Maisie McCracken. Suddenly, with the spring breeze ruffling his hair, he looked handsome and boyish.

"Attention, class. Ms. McCracken has had a good suggestion, I think. Instead of the historical walking tour we had scheduled after lunch, we're going to give you all the afternoon off."

The class erupted into cheers.

"The only rules are that you stay in groups of at least four," Ms. McCracken said. "I don't want anyone wandering around alone."

Everyone nodded. Most people were in groups already, and they began to buzz with conversation, trying to decide what to do. Screech noticed Nanny Parker standing alone. He quickly turned away before she decided to come over and torture him.

"If you need suggestions, I'd be happy to help out," Mr. Loomis said. "For example, I recommend a tour of the New York Public Library."

Everyone in the class nodded, as if this were a wonderful suggestion.

"Sounds awesome, Mr. Loomis," Slater said, and Mr. Loomis beamed.

As soon as Mr. Loomis and Ms. McCracken moved away, Slater turned back to the gang. "Okay, let's discuss reality. What should we do?"

"I think we should do what Ms. McCracken said and have fun," Zack said. "Let's try to forget about our troubles for the afternoon. We're in New York City—let's do something!"

"I think we should see a matinee of a musical," Slater volunteered. "Something with music and dancing."

"I agree about the matinee," Jessie said. "But I'd like to see a serious drama."

"But we're supposed to go to the theater tonight," Lisa argued. "I'd rather go shopping on Fifth Avenue."

"That sounds good to me," Kelly said. "What about you, Zack?"

"You girls shop every weekend in Palisades," Zack said. "Let's do something we can't do at home. How about the South Street Seaport? It's real historic—Mr. Loomis would like that—but it sounds fun, too. You can tour old ships, and there's a museum."

Lisa made a face. "I don't think I want to tour an old ship."

Zack sighed. "They have boutiques and shops, too."

"I'm with you, Zack," Lisa said quickly.

"Well," Screech said, "if we're going to tour ships, I think I'd rather go to the *Intrepid* on the Hudson River. It's a huge navy aircraft carrier." He coughed loudly.

"Maybe you should get some rest, Screech," Kelly said worriedly. "You sound like you're coming down with a cold."

"It's just a tickle in my throat," Screech said. "I feel fine."

"Wait," Lisa said. "I have some cough drops." She opened her purse and began to search inside. She frowned. "Whoops—it looks like they all spilled onto the bottom. Wait, here's one."

Lisa plucked out a gleaming red cough drop and held it out to Screech. Just then, it caught a ray of sun. The cough drop flashed, dazzling them for a minute. It gleamed in Lisa's hand with bloodred fire.

"Wait a second," Zack gasped. "That's no cough drop—that's a ruby!"

Dumbfounded, Lisa stared down at her hand. "Oh, my gosh," she said. "It's—"

"It's Auntie Marion's earring!" Screech squeaked.

Lisa screamed. Kelly weaved as though she would faint, and Screech fanned her and smashed her in the nose. Jessie took the ruby out of Lisa's hand and dropped it. When it rolled away, she crawled after it, bumping into Slater's knees. He fell over on top of the ruby and grabbed it.

"Calm down, gang!" Zack shouted. Everybody froze and looked at him. "We need to sit down and think," he said more calmly. "I suggest a restaurant. We might as well eat, right?"

"Now, *that's* what I call a plan," Slater said. "Let's go."

Planet Hollywood was only a few blocks away, so they walked there in silence. When they got inside, Zack leaned over and murmured, "Just act natural. Don't call attention to yourself."

Trying to act nonchalant, everyone followed the hostess. The restaurant was decorated with lots of props and costumes from Hollywood movies, but they were all too nervous to notice much. Even so, Screech got sidetracked when he recognized Dorothy's gingham dress from *The Wizard of Oz*. He stopped to peer over a seated woman's head at it, then tried to get even closer. But he bumped into a waiter, who was carrying a chef salad to the table. The salad upended right on the woman's head. She shrieked, and Screech scurried away as fast as he could.

"It's all your fault, Zack," Lisa said. "You *told* him to act natural."

They ordered cheeseburgers and shakes and tried to eat, but every time a police siren wailed outside, they jumped three feet in the air.

"Eat," Slater urged them. He was having no problem downing his cheeseburger and fries. "Brain cells need a major junk-food intake to operate."

"How would you know?" Jessie asked, stealing one of his fries. "You don't *have* any brain cells."

"I'm glad to see that things are getting back to normal," Zack said. "Now, while you were all not eating, I was coming up with a plan. This is what we're going to do. We're going to return Marion's earring."

Slater nodded. "That's a real good plan, preppy. Return it to Marion and apologize. I'm sure she'll forgive and forget. No problem."

"Slater's right," Kelly said. "She could still press charges. There's no way she'd believe it just dropped into Lisa's purse."

"That's why we have to return it without letting Marion Lenihan *know*," Zack answered. "We'll do it in a way that will make her think that she just misplaced it."

"How do we do *that*?" Kelly asked incredulously.

"We don't exactly travel in the same circles," Lisa said dourly.

"We got to her once; we can do it again," Zack said positively. "We just have to figure out where she'll be. That should be easy, since her social schedule is always in the gossip columns."

"That's true," Lisa said. "But I read this morning that she's cutting *back* on her social schedule because of the robbery. She canceled this dinner she was going to have at a fancy restaurant. If she never goes out of the house, how can we get to her?"

Zack gave them a sheepish grin. "That's the part of the plan I left to you guys to figure out," he said. "I can't do *everything*, you know."

▲   ▼   ▲

The one thing the gang agreed on was that the ruby earring had to remain safe at the hotel. At least one person would guard it at all times. Zack, Slater, and Screech volunteered to take the first shift, and they settled in to watch a sports event on cable.

Kelly, Jessie, and Lisa took the elevator down to the lobby. "What should we do?" Kelly asked.

"It's hard to think of anything when you're afraid you'll be arrested any minute," Jessie said.

"It's tough," Lisa agreed. Her brown eyes twinkled. "But you know what they say—when the going gets tough—"

"—the tough go shopping!" Kelly and Jessie finished.

"I definitely hear Bloomingdale's calling our names, girls," Lisa said. "Let's go."

When they hit the street, the doorman whistled for a cab, and one drove up right away.

"This is great," Lisa said as the doorman opened the cab door. "It's kind of like having your own limo, except it's yellow."

"And you don't have to worry about traffic or parking," Jessie agreed.

"I could get used to this," Kelly agreed as she shut the door. "Door-to-door service."

Just then, the cabdriver turned around. He had curly black hair and a crooked, infectious grin. "Where can I take you ladies?"

"I could *definitely* get used to this," Kelly murmured. *Why*, she thought, *he has the bluest eyes I've ever seen.*

"Bloomingdale's," Lisa said. "And take no prisoners. We're on a mission."

The driver laughed as he eased the cab into traffic. "Let me guess. You ladies are from out of town." His eyes met Kelly's in the mirror, and she felt a definite *zing*.

"California," she said faintly.

"I should have guessed. California has the most beautiful girls around," the driver said. He glanced into the mirror at Kelly again, and she felt that same *zing* again. But shouldn't all her *zings* be for *Zack*?

Jessie leaned forward to see the cabdriver's name. "Mitchell Tobias," she read. "Are you a native New Yorker, Mitchell?"

"Born and raised in Brooklyn," he said cheerfully. "And call me Mitch."

"How long have you driven a cab?" Lisa asked.

"Just about a year now," Mitch said. "After I graduated from Juilliard. I was a lousy waiter, so I decided this was my only option left. That is, until I'm starring on Broadway."

"You're an actor," Kelly blurted. What a stupid thing to say!

But Mitch didn't make fun of her. "That's right," he said as he coasted to a stop at a red light. "But as a working actor, I'm a good cabdriver, if you know what I mean."

"It must be hard," Kelly said sympathetically.

He turned. "It ain't easy. But it's the only life for me. And I've got plans. That's why I was hanging around your hotel."

"Why?" Kelly asked.

"A famous director is staying there," Mitch said. "His name is Max Springer, and he's had a major hit on Broadway practically every season for the past five years. He's one of the few directors around who can really *make* a star. I just know if I can only get him in my cab, I can impress him. I was thinking of doing Hamlet's soliloquy."

Jessie laughed. "I hope he's going more than a few blocks, then."

"I'll do it in double time, if it will impress him," Mitch vowed. "If he doesn't get into the cab this week, I'm going to try to crash the party he's throwing for his mother on Friday. She was a big movie star years ago named Sarah Springer, and he's organized this retrospective of her work at the Museum of Modern Art. He's kicking it off with a fancy cocktail party at the Metro. She made some dynamite films in the forties."

"I never heard of her," Kelly said.

"That's what can happen to actors," Mitch said. "They can have their moment, and then, poof, they're gone. You've got to keep your name out there, or everybody forgets you're alive."

"I'm sure you'll be successful, Mitch," Kelly said. *You're certainly cute enough to be a star.*

"All I need is my break," Mitch said. He pulled up in front of Bloomingdale's. "And *you* girls need some serious cash in this place. Have fun!"

"We will!" Lisa said, handing a bill to Mitch and telling him to keep the change.

Kelly said good-bye and good luck to Mitch. As she slid out of the seat, he gave her that special grin again. *Zing!*

She followed Lisa and Jessie onto the first floor of Bloomingdale's. An amazing array of merchandise met their eyes. Lisa was awed at the shoppers' flawless techniques. There was no wasted movement as they examined, considered, and whipped out their credit cards.

Lisa ran over to a display of silk scarves. She ran one through her fingers. "Did you ever see anything so gorgeous?" she asked Kelly.

Kelly looked at the azure blue scarf. It was the same color as Mitch's eyes. "Absolutely gorgeous," she agreed, swallowing hard.

She felt so guilty! Zack was sitting in a hotel room on this gorgeous spring day while she was mooning over a cabdriver. Zack was the only guy for her, Kelly told herself sternly as she picked up the scarf Lisa had let drop on the counter. He *was*. And as soon as she could push the thought of Mitch Tobias's blue eyes out of her mind, she was sure she'd remember it.

Chapter 7

▲ ▽ ▲ ▽ ▲ ▽ ▲

Screech felt he was getting on Zack's and Slater's nerves. But he couldn't help it—he *always* mixed up football and hockey! They both had goals, didn't they? Was it his fault when he asked when the quarterback was going to put on his skates?

Finally, Screech told them he was going for a walk. Zack and Slater didn't seem to mind a bit. He left the hotel and walked a few blocks until he saw an interesting-looking bookstore. Maybe he'd drop in and browse. He could use a good science-fiction book to read to take his mind off all this trouble with the ruby.

He was hoping for a stress-free half hour, but Screech found he was out of luck when he opened the door to the store and saw Nanny Parker. She was browsing through the celebrity biographies, and she saw Screech right away.

Screech nodded hello and went straight to the science fiction. A few seconds later, he felt someone by his side. Sure enough, it was Nanny.

"Hi," she said. "Looking for something in particular?"

"Nope," Screech said.

"Me, neither. I like to browse."

Screech moved down a few paces, and Nanny followed. He sighed and moved farther. Now he was in the cookbook section, but he took a book down and looked at it, anyway, hoping Nanny would go away.

"Did you and your friends crash that party at the museum yesterday?" she asked.

Screech looked up, annoyed. "Eavesdropping again? Do you have to be so nosy *all* the time?"

"I'm not nosy," Nanny said defensively, pushing her wire-rimmed glasses up the bridge of her nose. "I just notice things. I didn't eavesdrop. But you guys seemed really interested when I told you about Marion Lenihan's party. And then you got all dressed up just to go to the museum. And then you disappeared right in the middle of the Impressionists. And you all looked really nervous when you came back. So I just fit the pieces together."

"Well, it's none of your business," Screech said. But he had to admit he *did* admire Nanny's powers of observation.

"I know," Nanny said with a sigh. "That's my

trouble, though. I like to know what's going on. So how was the party, anyway?"

"I didn't get in," Screech said shortly.

"Oh." He could tell Nanny was dying to ask him if anybody else did, but she didn't. She just picked up a cookbook and leafed through it casually.

"You know, I've never had cappuccino," she said. "Isn't that funny? Because I love coffee. I think coffee ice cream is my favorite. What's yours?"

"Do you *always* talk so much?" Screech asked.

"Yeah, sure. I have a lot to say. Have you ever had cappuccino?"

"No," Screech said.

"Do you want to come with me and get some?" Nanny asked. "There's this neat cappuccino bar in the lobby of our hotel. They have pastries, too."

Screech was just about to look up and say *"No way, José."* Why should he go anywhere with Nanny Parker after she'd trashed his reputation as a ladies' man at Bayside High? But a funny thing happened when he looked at her. Behind her glasses, her light brown eyes looked soft and eager. She looked almost pretty in a plain way. Or was it plain in a pretty way? Anyway, it was too bad she had such a rotten personality.

Suddenly, Screech wondered why Nanny was browsing in a bookstore all by herself. She was supposed to stay with a group this afternoon, and it wasn't like her to disobey a teacher. It was because she didn't *have* anyone to pal around with, Screech realized. *She's lonely*, he thought.

So he found himself saying what he never imagined he could say. "I guess I can. If it doesn't take too long."

Nanny brightened. "Great! Let's go."

They walked back onto the street and headed to the hotel. "I love New York," Nanny said. "I want to work here someday. My dream is to have my very own column in a New York paper. I want to be a famous journalist like Billy Cahill. I've sent him some clippings of my column and written him a couple of fan letters. I'm sure he'll write back to me any day now."

"A gossip columnist isn't a journalist," Screech said disdainfully.

"Sure he is," Nanny said. "News *is* gossip, Screech. It's people finding out what other people are up to. News is gossip, and gossip is news."

"No, it's people prying into other people's private lives," Screech said.

"Well, if they're famous, why shouldn't people know stuff about them?" Nanny countered. "They make money off the public. Anyway, as I was saying, it's super hard to get your own column. I'd have to come up with a really great scoop to break in."

"I'm sure with your technique you'll be able to," Screech said sourly.

"Thanks," Nanny said brightly.

As they pushed open the doors of the lobby and started toward the stairs to the second tier of the lobby, Nanny put her hand on Screech's arm.

"Look, Screech," she whispered. "Isn't that the homeless woman we saw yesterday?"

Screech looked over. It *was* the same woman. She must have gotten up the courage to come into the lobby. She was wearing the same old raincoat and sneakers from the day before, and a security guard was asking her questions. She was looking down at the floor in an embarrassed way.

"The poor woman," Nanny murmured. "She looks really miserable."

"Follow me," Screech said. He crossed the lobby briskly and went right up to the woman. "Aunt Sonia!" he cried. "We're so sorry we're late." He looked the guard in the eye. "Is there a problem, sir?"

"Not at all," the guard said, backing away. "Sorry, ma'am."

The woman looked at Screech and Nanny. "Thank you," she said in a dignified way.

"We were just about to get some cappuccino," Screech said. "Would you like to join us?"

"No, really—"

"We'd really like it if you would," Nanny said. "We want to meet real New Yorkers, but it's kind of hard. You can't just stop people on the street and ask them how they are."

The woman smiled. "In that case, I'd be happy to."

They went upstairs and sat at a little café table. The woman ordered a cappuccino, but Screech and Nanny decided to try a café mocha, which was cappuccino with chocolate and whipped cream. Screech also ordered an assorted pastry tray with the coffees.

"I guess we should introduce ourselves," the woman said. "I'm Sally."

"I'm Samuel, but everybody calls me Screech," Screech said. "And this is Nanny."

"I guess you're wondering why I keep hanging around this place," the woman said.

"You don't have to tell us," Screech said.

"But we'd love to know," Nanny said quickly.

Sally stirred her cappuccino slowly. "Someone I . . . used to know is staying here. Part of me wants to say hello to him. And part of me is afraid."

"Someone you used to know," Nanny said thoughtfully. Her brown eyes narrowed. "You mean someone you used to love," she guessed.

Screech couldn't believe it. Now Nanny was going to pry into the secrets of a complete stranger! He gave her a dirty look, but Nanny ignored it.

Sally's pale blue eyes held a faraway gaze. "Yes," she said. "I haven't seen him in twenty years. The last time I saw him was in a restaurant here in New York. He was with his wife and daughter. He didn't see me. I know his wife died a few years ago. But now, I don't think it's a good idea to see him again. I've changed so much. I'm just going to go home."

Sally looked so sad that Screech felt like his heart would break. "Would you like one of these little pastry things?" he asked, offering her the plate.

Sally shook her head, smiling. "That's called a cannoli," she said. "I grew up in Greenwich Village here in New York, so I know a lot about Italian pastry."

"I've heard a lot about Greenwich Village," Nanny said. "It's not on our scheduled list of stops, though."

"But you must go there!" Sally cried. "It's the best part of New York. There're wonderful little alleys to explore, and cafés, and bookstores, and Washington Square Park. . . ."

"It would be nice if a native New Yorker would show it to us," Nanny said. "Like you, for instance. Do you have some free time?"

Sally looked startled. Then she smiled a lovely smile that made Screech realize she must have been very pretty once. "As a matter of fact, I do," she said.

▲   ▼   ▲

That night, the class was scheduled to see a Broadway play. They had bought the tickets a month in advance. Everyone was looking forward to it, but the gang had a problem—what about the ruby? Somebody had to stay home and watch it.

"I'll stay," Jessie said.

"Me, too," Slater said quickly.

Lisa gazed at them incredulously. "Hold on. You guys were the ones who were dying to go to the theater. You don't want to miss the play tonight."

Jessie gave a big yawn. "All that shopping today really tired me out."

"And I went up to the health club to work out," Slater said. "I'm beat. I wouldn't mind ordering room service and catching a movie on cable."

"Me, either," Jessie said. The two looked at each other, then looked away.

"Are you sure you don't mind?" Kelly asked dubiously. "I could stay. I'm used to baby-sitting, that's for sure."

"We don't mind," Slater and Jessie said together.

"But we're going to this great Italian restaurant in the theater district before the show," Zack said. "I know how Slater likes to eat. I could stay."

"No way," Jessie said. "You and Kelly need some time together."

"Well," Kelly said, "if you're *sure*. . . ."

"We're sure!" Jessie trilled. "Now go on, get

moving. The reservations are for six-thirty, and you know how Mr. Loomis is about being prompt!"

She and Slater stood together and waved good-bye to the rest of the gang as they filed out of the room. The door clicked shut behind them.

Jessie turned to Slater. They grinned and fell into each other's arms.

"I thought they'd never leave," Slater said.

▲   ▼   ▲

After a terrific meal of garlic bread and lasagna, Kelly and Zack left the restaurant ahead of the others and strolled to the theater, hand in hand.

"Jessie was right," Zack said. "It's nice to have some time alone. Especially when in another few minutes, we'll be sitting with twenty of our closest friends."

Kelly laughed. "I'm having a really good time. If only I didn't freak out every time a police car goes by."

"Try not to think about it tonight," Zack urged. "Tomorrow we'll look at the gossip columns and try to find out what Marion is doing. If not, I'll think of something else. So tonight, just concentrate on having fun."

"I *am* having fun," Kelly said. She looked up at the theater marquee and wondered how Mitch's name would look up in lights. Had he seen this play? He probably went to all the Broadway plays, Kelly thought with a sigh. It would be so much fun to talk to him about them!

"What's the matter, Kelly?" Zack asked, squeezing her hand.

"Oh. Nothing. I was just thinking how much fun it would be to live in New York." *And date someone like Mitch*, Kelly thought.

"Yeah, I was thinking that, too," Zack agreed. *And date someone like Alex.*

They gave their tickets to the usher and settled into their seats. While they were reading their programs, Kelly leaned over and pointed to a restaurant ad. "That's Marion Lenihan's favorite place," she whispered to Zack. "I read it in the paper. The owner was real upset when she canceled the dinner party and decided to hold it at her private club instead."

Her private club. Suddenly, Zack had a brainstorm. How could he have forgotten? Alex Washburne said that she worked at Marion's private club. He could get to Marion that way! Alex had already invited him to tour the kitchen.

He opened his mouth to tell Kelly but then closed it. How could he tell Kelly that the reason he'd returned late from the party was because he'd met another girl? She'd be furious.

It was his fault Kelly was in this mess, and he'd

have to get her out. And if he had to see the adorable Alex Washburne again to do it, well, that was the price he'd have to pay. Because he'd do anything for Kelly—even if it meant sneaking behind her back to see another gorgeous girl. *I'll just have to make the sacrifice*, Zack thought. *That's the kind of guy I am.*

Chapter 8

▲ ▼ ▲ ▼ ▲ ▼ ▲

Screech had ordered two desserts at the restaurant, an Italian ice cream called *gelato* and chocolate mousse, so he was left behind finishing up every bite. He had to race to catch up to the others at the theater.

When he got there, he saw that the seat next to Nanny was empty. Before he went to his own assigned seat, he slipped into the one next to her.

Nanny gave him a pleased smile. "Hi."

"I just wanted to show you something," Screech said.

Nanny's face fell. "Oh." Then she smiled again. "You know, I had the best time today. I love Greenwich Village. And Sally knew so much of the history there. I'd rather listen to *her* than Mr. Loomis any day. She had some great stories. Remember the one about New Year's Eve in nineteen thirty-two when she got everyone in that café to go to Washington Square Park to dance?"

"Yeah," Screech said.

"And it was so sad when she was telling us about her lost love," Nanny said with a sigh. "She thought she'd be bad for his career. I wonder why she didn't tell us what he did. And she never even told him she loved him. It is *so* sad."

"Yeah," Screech said. "Can I say something now?"

"Sure," Nanny said. "But I just want to tell you that I had a really good time today."

"Me, too," Screech said. He *had* had fun. It was probably because Nanny hadn't talked a mile a minute all day. Sally was so interesting that Nanny had just listened for a change.

Screech reached into his pocket and took out a twenty-dollar bill. "Look what I found in my pocket when I got home."

"What's that?" Nanny asked. "A tip?"

"It's the twenty-dollar bill I slipped into Sally's pocket the other morning when we first met her," Screech explained. "She must have put it in my pocket this afternoon when I wasn't looking."

"Wow," Nanny said. "She's really something. I wish there was something we could do for her. She seems so poor and lonesome. It's funny how she won't tell us where she lives or anything. I think she's homeless, Screech."

"I do, too," Screech agreed. The houselights

dimmed, and he started to rise. "I'd better go to my seat."

"Why don't you just sit here?" Nanny suggested. "It was Mr. Loomis's seat, but he took Jessie's instead. I think he wanted to sit next to Ms. McCracken. It's too dark to find your seat, anyway," she pointed out.

"Oh," Screech said. Slowly, he sat down again. "I guess I might as well." *Great.* Now he had to sit next to Nanny Parker for two whole hours! As the curtain rose, Screech consoled himself with the thought that at least she'd have to keep her mouth shut.

▲   ▼   ▲

Later, back at the hotel, Jessie stood up as soon as the credits began to roll on the movie they'd watched.

"I'd better get back to my room," she said. "Kelly and Lisa will think it's weird if I'm not there when they get back." She grinned and tossed her long ponytail behind her shoulder. "They wouldn't believe that we could be together for so long without having a fight."

Slater grabbed for her hand. "That's because I kept you in a lip lock," he teased. His dimples deepened as he grinned. "It was a sacrifice, but I was up to the task."

Jessie returned his smile, but suddenly, she frowned.

"What is it?" Slater asked. "I was only kidding. I had a really good time tonight, Jess."

"It's not that," Jessie said. "I just thought of how hard it will be to tell everyone that we're back together. I swore on my copy of *One Hundred Ways to a Healthy Planet* that I'd never go out with you again. Kelly and Lisa saw me do it."

"Tell me about it," Slater groaned. "I told Zack I'd give him my car if I ever asked you out again."

"Zack is right," Jessie said. "We *should* be part of some psychological study. I've had more break-ups than Elizabeth Taylor. And they're all with the same guy!" She covered her face with her hands. "It's so embarrassing. Can you imagine what Nanny Parker will say in her column?"

"Who cares?" Slater asked. But he winced when he thought of the ribbing he'd get at school. "Look, I have a plan," he said after a minute.

Jessie grinned. "You sound like Zack. This definitely means trouble."

"No way," Slater said. "It's real simple—we don't tell anybody we got back together."

Jessie looked doubtful. "How can we do that?"

"Easy," Slater said. "We keep our mouths shut."

Jessie thought about this. It might not be such a bad idea. It would take the pressure off them, for one thing. They could actually have an argument without the whole school taking out bets about whether they'd break up. And if they *did* break up—not that Jessie thought they *would*, but then again, their track record wasn't exactly stellar—nobody would have to know but them.

"Do you really think we can do it?" she asked Slater doubtfully.

Slater nodded. "Just think. It might be kind of fun." He twined his fingers through hers.

"A clandestine relationship," Jessie murmured.

"No, just a secret one," Slater said.

She rolled her eyes. "That's what I just said."

"No, that's what *I* just said."

Jessie giggled and leaned over to brush her lips against his. "I'd better say good night before we break up again."

"So we'll keep this a secret?" Slater asked.

"Our secret," Jessie agreed.

▲   ▼   ▲

The next morning, the girls felt too lazy to get up for breakfast. But after looking at the room-service prices, they decided that one of them should go for takeout from the deli across the street. Kelly volunteered to be the one.

She pulled on her jeans and left on the old blue T-shirt she'd slept in. She didn't bother brushing her hair but threw on the baseball cap Zack had left in their room.

So it was her very own fault when she pushed through the steel doors of the hotel and saw Mitch Tobias leaning against the door of his cab. He was reading the paper, and Kelly stopped dead in her tracks, uncertain whether to say hello or run the other way. She looked so awful!

But she didn't get a chance to decide. Mitch looked up and saw her. He grinned the lopsided grin that turned her to mush, then tossed the newspaper back into the cab and came toward her.

"I was hoping I'd see you again," he said.

"You were?" Kelly blurted. "I mean, hi."

"So where are you off to so early? It can't be a baseball game," he said, indicating her hat with a smile. "The Yanks are still in spring training."

"I volunteered to get breakfast for Jessie and Lisa," Kelly explained. She wished she'd at least brushed her hair. And she didn't care about not having any makeup on, but she could have at least put on some lip gloss!

"Well, now I know your friends' names," Mitch said. "What about yours?"

"Kelly."

"So, Kelly, what are your plans?"

"Gee, I don't know," Kelly said. "I guess college next year and—"

Mitch laughed. "I was talking about breakfast. Where are you going to pick it up?"

Kelly blushed crimson. "Oh. At the deli across the street."

"I have a better idea," Mitch said. "Hop in the cab and I'll take you to a place that makes the best muffins in the world. Great coffee, too. Cabdrivers always know the best places." When she hesitated, he said, "It's not far, just a few blocks away. You'll be back in five minutes."

"Okay," Kelly said. She hopped into the front seat of the cab.

Mitch started the engine. "You know, you're really pretty in the morning," he said. "You look adorable in that hat."

And suddenly, seeing the approval in Mitch's eyes, Kelly felt like the most beautiful girl in all of New York City. *Who needs lip gloss?* she thought happily.

While Mitch drove, Kelly asked him what it was like to be a struggling actor in New York City. He told her funny stories about his disastrous career as a waiter, his acting classes, and about his friends, who were all, like him, waiting for their big break.

Kelly ordered blueberry muffins and coffee from a dour waitress who broke into a smile when she saw Mitch. Everybody in the coffee shop seemed to know him, and they traded gossip and friendly insults back and forth. It was amazing, Kelly thought as she hopped back in the cab. She'd never dreamed New York could be such a friendly place!

She was sorry when Mitch pulled up in front of the Metro Hotel. Kelly wanted to linger, but she knew that Jessie and Lisa were starving, and the coffee was getting cold.

"Thanks a lot, Mitch," she said as she opened the door of the cab.

"Listen," Mitch said, "what are you doing tonight?"

Kelly's heart beat faster. "We have a free night," she said. "Some of the class is going to a jazz club, but my friends haven't decided yet."

"A friend of mine is giving this party downtown," Mitch said. "Just a bunch of disreputable actors, but it should be fun. Why don't you come? Your friends, too, of course."

"I don't know . . . ," Kelly said hesitantly.

"Here's the address," Mitch said, scribbling it on the edge of the newspaper and tearing it off. "The party starts at eight. If you can, stop by." He handed her the paper, and his fingers brushed hers. "I'd really like to see you again, Kelly."

Kelly felt like she was going to faint with happiness. He wanted to see her again! "I'll try to make it," she said. She slid out of the cab just as the doorman whistled for a cab for a hotel guest. Mitch coasted forward, the passenger got in, and he took off.

Kelly stood there, holding the bag of muffins and coffee. She felt exhilarated and dizzy and confused—all the feelings she once had had for Zack.

Just then, Zack pushed open the lobby doors.

"Hey, Kelly! Whoa," he said when he saw her appearance. He grinned. "Did you just fall out of bed and roll down the stairs?" He gave her cap a tug.

He was teasing her, of course. But he made Kelly feel like a pair of old tennis shoes. And Mitch— Mitch had told her how pretty she was, and he had made her feel wonderful.

▲   ▼   ▲

That morning, the class went on a Circle Line cruise around Manhattan. It was a beautiful day, clear and warm, and the fresh breeze felt good against their faces. And it sure helped that Mr. Loomis didn't bore them too much with more stories about what had happened in New York City during the revolutionary war. He was too busy sitting with Maisie McCracken.

Kelly sat with Lisa and Jessie and watched the city slip by while she told them what had happened with Mitch that morning. When she told them about the party, they really got excited.

"We just have to go!" Lisa exclaimed. "We'd really be sorry if we missed out on a real New York party. And I'm tired of feeling so stressed out about being a jewel thief. I keep hoping it will all blow over. I've been crossing my fingers all morning. You can't *believe* how hard it was to do my nails."

"A party does sound like fun," Jessie agreed. "I bet that really interesting people will be there."

"I know," Kelly admitted. "It sounds fantastic."

Lisa poked Kelly gently. "So what's the problem, girlfriend? Is it Mitch?"

"I thought you liked him," Jessie said, confused.

Lisa gave Jessie an incredulous look. "Of course she *likes* him. That's the whole problem. Or should I say the problem is a *who*, not a *what*."

"Huh?" Jessie asked.

"Not *huh*," Lisa said. "*Who*. Zack." She turned to Kelly. "Let me guess. It's not that you don't want Zack there. But you don't want Zack there."

"Lisa, one of these days, you're going to have to make sense when you talk," Jessie complained. "I don't know if I can take much more of this."

"Actually, she *is* making sense," Kelly said, biting her lip. "I feel awful. I really do love Zack. But I really want to see Mitch! If Zack comes to the party, I won't get a chance to talk to Mitch at all. I feel so guilty!"

"But you can't miss out on the party!" Jessie said. "That would be stupid."

"Not to mention it would mean that *we'd* miss out on it," Lisa said.

"Wait a second," Jessie said. "I just remembered. Zack volunteered to stay home and baby-sit the ruby tonight."

"Zack told you that?" Kelly asked.

"No, Slater did," Jessie explained.

"When did you talk to Slater?" Lisa asked curiously.

"On the subway this morning," Jessie said quickly. Actually, she and Slater had arranged to meet in the lobby before anyone else came down. "Anyway," she said quickly, "since Zack is staying home, we can all go to the party."

"But I'd feel terrible," Kelly said.

Zack walked over, eating a hot dog. "Why all the doom and gloom, girls? I know we still have a ruby problem, but I think Screech is a pretty reliable baby-sitter. And I don't see any police boats around."

"We've been invited to a party tonight," Lisa said. "The other day, we met this cute—I mean, this really nice cabdriver. He's a real New York actor. He invited us to a party downtown."

"Sounds like fun," Zack said, finishing his hot dog. "Sorry I'll miss it." *Not really,* Zack thought. *I'll be seeing Alex instead.* He'd already called her this morning and invited himself to the Washington Irving Club tonight. It was the night of Marion Lenihan's party.

"But don't you want to come?" Kelly asked him.

Zack shrugged. "Sure. But I already volunteered, and it's only fair. Slater missed the theater last night, and Screech missed the cruise today." He patted Kelly's shoulder. "Don't worry about me."

Kelly smiled up at him, but she felt miserable. Zack was being so nice, and she was going off to a party to meet another guy! It wasn't like she had a date or anything. But she was still a horrible person, Kelly thought. She felt like telling Zack about Mitch right then and there, but she couldn't. Why should she hurt Zack when she'd be flying back to Palisades with him and wouldn't ever see Mitch again?

Zack saw how sad Kelly looked. She had really wanted him to go to the party, poor thing. He felt terrible, and he felt like confessing his date with Alex Washburne right then and there. But it wasn't really a date, he rationalized. And besides, they'd be leaving New York in three days.

Zack sat next to Kelly and slipped his arm around her as they rounded the bottom of Manhattan Island. Kelly leaned against him so that he couldn't see the guilty expression on her face.

I can't tell her, Zack thought.

I can't tell him, Kelly reasoned.

Daisy Tyler and Vivian Mahoney walked by at that moment. Daisy gazed at Zack and Kelly, a misty look in her baby blue eyes. "Just look, Vivian," she said with a sigh. "Aren't they just the perfect couple?"

Chapter 9

▲ ▼ ▲ ▼ ▲ ▼ ▲

Zack nervously straightened his tie as he approached the Washington Irving Club. It was a large, imposing brownstone with a high, wrought-iron gate. Mellow lamplight peeked out through heavy drapes on the front windows, and a brass plaque announced it had been founded in 1889. It looked classy and intimidating, but Alex had told him not to worry, just to tell the doorman he was her guest.

Somehow Zack had been worried that he'd be thrown out on the street, but as soon as he spoke Alex Washburne's name, the forbidding look on the doorman's face cleared and he waved Zack on through, giving him instructions to the kitchen.

Zack felt like his feet would sink into the carpet. Crystal chandeliers sparkled over his head, and shaded lamps illuminated rooms off the hallway, which shone with burnished bronze statues and dark walnut paneling. Thick draperies shut out the noise of the busy Manhattan street.

Zack walked through an empty reception room, pushed open a door, and went down a short hall-way. Now he could hear the muffled sounds of the clattering of pots and pans. He could also hear someone yelling in a French accent. Zack hesitated in front of the double doors leading to the kitchen. The doors almost hit him in the nose when they were flung open and Alex rushed out.

She looked adorable in black pants, a white shirt, and a long butcher's apron. Her wild, fuzzy curls were tamed in a French braid, but a few little wisps escaped around her ears. Zack started to smile, but then he noticed that Alex looked upset.

"Oh, Zack, you're here!" she said, taking his arm and leading him a little way down the hall. "It's a disaster," she said in a low, worried voice. "Marion Lenihan is throwing a dinner party. It's small—only sixteen people—but it's *crucial* that everything go right. And two of the waiters didn't show up! They decided to elope to Europe together. The chef is furious. We all have to pitch in."

Alex looked up at him with worried amber eyes. "I'm afraid I can't give you the tour of the kitchen tonight. Antoine is a nervous wreck. Never mind Antoine, *I'm* a nervous wreck."

Zack had to laugh at Alex's frazzled expression. "Don't worry about me," he assured her. "It's fine." As a matter of fact, this could fit in even better with his plans. Thank goodness it hadn't been one of the cooks who had run out. Zack might have had to offer to help out, and there's no way he could walk into a kitchen and pretend to be a chef. But he could probably handle helping out in the dining room. That might get him close to the Lenihan table. "Let me help out, Alex," he said.

She gave him an incredulous look. "But we're shorthanded in the dining room. That means clearing plates and filling water glasses—that kind of thing."

"Right up my alley," Zack said.

"But, Zack, you're a chef. I can't ask you to clear plates!"

"You're not asking; I'm offering," Zack said firmly. "And how do you think I started out in the first place?"

Alex reached out and squeezed his arm. "You are really something special, Zack," she said softly. "Most chefs are such *snobs*. But you're just a regular guy."

"That's absolutely right, Alex," Zack said. "I *am* just a regular guy." *More than you know.*

"Come on," Alex said. "I'll get you an apron and show you the ropes. I hope you won't regret this!"

Alex took off down the hall. She moved faster than half the guys on his track team. Zack followed her to a pantry, where she gave him an apron and shoved a pitcher of water into his hands.

"Mrs. Lenihan is in the small private dining room," she said. "Just fill all the water glasses and come back here. I'll have the bread baskets together by then."

"Wait a second, Alex," Zack said. "You want me to help you with the *Lenihan* table?"

"Sure," Alex said. "That's where we need the help. Don't worry; you'll be fine."

"Fine," Zack gulped. He hadn't expected to be stuck in a tiny room with Marion Lenihan. He just hoped she wouldn't recognize him without Kelly and Lisa. And maybe she wouldn't notice him since he was dressed like a waiter.

Alex pointed to the door of the private dining room and gave him an encouraging smile. Zack pushed it open cautiously and stepped out. He was behind Marion, who was sitting regally at the head of the table. By her feet was a small red purse that Zack recognized from the other night. All he'd have to do was somehow open it and slip the ruby into it. And he'd have to do it while keeping his face away from her at all times.

Zack started to fill the water glasses. He maneuvered closer and closer to Marion while conversation swirled around him. He kept his head down and concentrated on keeping his hand steady so that he wouldn't spill a drop.

Stay cool, Zack told himself. After tonight, he

could end up a hero. Zack winced, nearly spilling water on Marion's hand. He moved quickly away. *Or I could end up in jail!*

▲   ▼   ▲

"Are you *sure* this is the address?" Lisa asked Kelly.

"I'm sure," Kelly said. She looked up at the building dubiously. It looked more like a factory than an apartment building. They were in a warehouse district of downtown New York, and it was pretty dark and spooky.

Jessie looked around nervously. "Maybe we should have asked the cab to wait."

"Come on, girls," Slater said. "Don't be wimps. We're feeling adventurous, remember?"

"Is that what I'm feeling?" Screech asked. "I thought it was fear."

Slater laughed. "Let's not stand here all night. Let's ring the buzzer."

Kelly pressed 5C and heard the sharp buzz that meant they could open the door. They peered inside at a dimly lit stairway. "This is getting worse and worse," Lisa said.

"Well, we're here," Kelly said nervously. "We might as well go on up."

When they reached the fifth floor, they didn't

need to peer at the numbers. They could hear the reassuring sounds of music and laughter coming from the door at the far end. Kelly rang the bell and nervously smoothed her hair. She hoped that Mitch was already there. She'd never had to enter a party where she didn't know anyone before.

A stranger opened the door, a tall redheaded guy wearing a top hat. "Welcome!" he said. Behind him, Kelly could see a huge open space filled with people.

"We're friends of Mitch's," Kelly explained.

"You can come in, anyway," the young guy joked. "I'm Presley. Mitch is in my acting class. He's here someplace. Sodas are in the bathtub, and you have to dive for the chips."

"Thanks," Kelly said. She looked around dazedly. The furniture in the loft looked like it had been picked up off the street, but it was painted in cheerful primary colors. The lumpy couch was full of pillows that were covered in a colorful fabric that looked like it came from the forties. Someone was playing a grand piano, and everywhere people were talking animatedly and laughing at each other's jokes.

"Wow," Lisa said. "This looks like a fun party."

"Everyone looks so *interesting*," Jessie murmured. "And older. I hope we fit in."

"This sure isn't Palisades," Slater agreed.

"It sure isn't," Screech said. "Nobody has a tan."

Kelly saw Mitch heading through the crowd, waving at them. He looked super happy to see them. "You came!" he said. "I'm really glad."

Kelly introduced him to Slater and Screech, and Mitch led them to the bathtub, which was in the kitchen.

"This is really weird," Lisa said as she took a soda. "What do you do when you have to take a bath?"

"Presley has a screen that fits around the tub," Mitch explained.

"I think it's a great idea," Screech said. "You can take the dishes into the tub with you and wash *them* and yourself at the same time!"

Mitch laughed. "I stayed here for a while until I had my own place. It's great. It's hard to get a place with this much room in New York. Come on, let me introduce you around."

He led them across the loft to an energetic group standing by the tall windows. "Everybody, I want you to meet some friends of mine from California," Mitch said. "This is Kelly, Lisa, Jessie, Slater, and Screech." Then he went around the circle and introduced his friends.

"Pretty impressive, Mitch," Slater said. "You just met us and you remembered all our names."

"I'm an actor," Mitch said with an easygoing grin. "A good memory is something you work on."

"Endlessly," a tall blond woman named Nancy

said. "Now, what did you just say, Mitch?"

Everybody laughed. "Hey," Mitch said to Kelly, "I forgot to ask if you were hungry. There's chips and guacamole."

"At least *that's* the same as California," Lisa whispered to Screech.

Presley turned to Kelly. "Even if you're starving, I wouldn't let Mitch fetch you anything. You'll end up with guacamole all over your clothes."

"Mitch was the worst waiter in the world," Nancy said. "Diners would see him coming and hide under the tables."

"Hey!" Mitch protested amiably. "I wasn't that bad." Everyone groaned, and he added, "Well, I guess it's safer for New York if I stay in my cab."

"I wish I could drive a cab," a short, cute girl named Angela said. "I have to walk for a living."

"Walk?" Kelly asked.

"Dogs," Mitch explained. "You'd be surprised what actors do to survive. Dean washes dishes in a Chinese restaurant. Andy tends bar. Nancy is a waitress, and Devon gives piano lessons to kids. We have to have jobs that have flexible schedules, so we can go to auditions."

"It must be really tough," Kelly sympathized.

"Tell me about it," Nancy said. "I get home at midnight, and I can barely get my feet out of my shoes and tomato sauce out of my hair."

"You should try walking ten dogs at a time,"

Angela said. "Listening to them bark drives me crazy. These rich people should spend some money on training their pets. I have this one dog called Pookie—you can't believe how nasty this little puppy is. Of course, one of the richest women in New York raised it. All I can say is, I'd hate to see her kids. Marion Lenihan is a real witch."

"Marion Lenihan!" Kelly exclaimed.

Angela made a face. "The queen herself. I can't tell you how glad I am that I got that sitcom in L.A. On Friday, I'm going to kiss those dogs good-bye."

"Sounds like fun," Presley said. "Can I come? I haven't had a date in months."

While the rest of the group burst out laughing, Kelly, Lisa, Jessie, Slater, and Screech exchanged glances. They'd all had the same idea. Could precious little Pookie be the answer they were looking for?

▲   ▼   ▲

Zack got chance after chance, and he blew every one. First, someone knocked over Marion's purse. But when he went to pick it up, the man on her left reached it first. Then, just as Zack had dropped a napkin and bent down to swipe the purse, Marion picked it up and went to the ladies' room.

Zack peeked out through the door of the pantry.

Dessert was over, everyone had finished their coffee, and Marion was still seated, saying her good-byes. The evening was almost over. If he didn't seize his chance, he'd never get another one.

Marion reached for her purse and snapped it open. She got out a compact and began to powder her nose, leaving the purse open on an empty chair next to her.

Perfect! Quickly, Zack pushed open the door and moved swiftly toward the table. He reached into his pocket and took out the ruby. Concealing it in his fist, he maneuvered closer to the table. He took aim carefully. He'd have to pitch it in a perfect arc.

Zack took a couple of steps closer. But on his last step, he tripped over the end of the carpet and pitched forward. He grabbed a chair to steady himself, which shot forward and knocked over a coffee cup. The coffee spilled all over Mrs. Lenihan's jeweled compact.

"Oh, no!" she cried. "The powder is ruined!" She looked up and stared straight at Zack. "That was very clumsy of you, young—"

"Sorry," Zack said quickly, starting to move away.

Suddenly, Marion screamed. "It's him! It's him! Stop, thief!"

Zack didn't have time to think. One of the guests reached out to grab him, but he leaped the extra foot and practically fell through the pantry door. Regaining his balance, he dashed past a shocked Alex toward the kitchen. He raced through the kitchen, upending a tray full of silverware, which crashed to the floor. Zack nimbly jumped over the bouncing forks, wrenched open the back door, and ran into the alley. He dived behind a bunch of garbage cans.

In another minute, he heard the door open and footsteps on the landing.

"He's not out here," he heard Alex say. "He must have left through the alley gate. We've lost him."

The door closed again, but Zack stayed behind the cans. He wasn't about to risk being seen. He slipped his hand inside his pocket to make sure the ruby was safe. It wasn't there, so he checked the other pocket. Zack felt faint. This couldn't be happening. The ruby was gone!

Chapter 10

▲　▼　▲　▼　▲　▼　▲

The moon was so bright and full, it seemed to be suspended over their heads like a luminous ball. Kelly sat on the fire-escape steps with Mitch, talking softly. The party was winding down, but she didn't want to leave. She felt suspended tonight, as though there were no yesterdays and no tomorrows. All she wanted to do was sit here on the warm steps, underneath the moon, and talk to Mitch.

She'd had such a good time tonight. All of Mitch's friends were so interesting and fun. They were full of ambition and fun. Kelly had never thought she'd like to live in a huge city like New York or even leave California. But suddenly she could see herself there. Maybe she could take acting lessons. It would be fun to go to class and then sit in cafés talking about plays with her fellow students. It would be a blast to get half-price tickets to Broadway plays and sit in the balcony. And it would be super romantic to do it with Mitch.

"I've had a fantastic time tonight," Mitch said softly. "I'm really glad you and your friends decided to go to Bloomingdale's yesterday."

"Me, too," Kelly said. "Thank you for inviting us tonight. Everyone's had a really good time."

"Well, I'm glad your friends have enjoyed themselves," Mitch said. "But I have to admit that I really only wanted to see you."

Kelly held her breath. Mitch was gazing at her so intently. His blue eyes looked as dark as the midnight sky. He leaned over. He was going to kiss her! Kelly held her breath.

"Kelly!" Lisa poked her sleepy head through the window. "I think we'd better head back. If I drink another soda, I'm going to float away. Screech is asleep in the bathtub, and Jessie and Slater are so tired, they're not even arguing."

Kelly sprang to her feet. "I'm ready."

Behind her, Mitch grabbed her hand. "Are you sure you can't stay?" he whispered as Lisa withdrew her head.

Kelly turned. "I'd like to," she admitted softly. "But I can't."

Mitch rose. "Okay. But I hope there's a next time. Come on, I'll help you guys find a cab. We should probably walk over to Hudson Street."

The streets were quiet as they walked a few blocks over to a busy intersection. Kelly was disappointed when a cab appeared almost immediately. Mitch only had time to squeeze her hand before settling her inside.

"I'll see you tomorrow," he told her. "If you need a ride anywhere, I'm available."

Kelly smiled. "Okay."

As the cab pulled away, Lisa turned to her. "So did you talk to Mitch about his friend Angela?"

"Angela?" Kelly asked, watching Mitch get smaller through the back window of the cab.

"The girl who walks Marion's dog," Lisa said impatiently. "We have to find out more so that we can come up with a plan."

"That's right," Kelly said. "I forgot all about it."

"Oh, well," Lisa said, yawning. "I'm too tired to think about it now. We can talk about it tomorrow."

They reached the hotel with only five minutes to spare before curfew. They hurried to the elevator and took it to their floor. Now that they were going to see Zack, Kelly felt guilty all over again. She'd forgotten all about him for the whole night!

But when they opened the door to the room, Zack wasn't there.

"This is weird," Slater said with a frown. "Zack said he was going to eat in the room and catch a movie on cable." He walked over to the dresser drawer, opened it, and unwrapped a pair of socks.

He turned and gazed at them, wide-eyed. "The ruby is gone!"

▲   ▼   ▲

Zack looked at his watch again. He'd been sitting behind the garbage cans for fifteen minutes, and he was starting to wonder what to do. He hadn't heard any police sirens, and nobody had come out of the club. Should he risk coming out?

There was no way he could leave without looking for the ruby inside. He figured it must have flown out of his fingers when he tripped over the rug. With all the excitement, he hadn't noticed.

Just then, he heard the bang of the back door. Zack hunched down behind the cans. He heard footsteps coming closer and closer. Then a plastic bag of garbage swung and hit him in the head.

"What do you know," Alex drawled flatly. "A rat."

Zack peeked at her. "Hi."

"Don't worry, you're safe," Alex said. "You can come out. I covered for you."

Zack got to his feet. "Alex, you're incredible," he said fervently. "Thank you."

"Can the flattery," Alex said crisply. "Of course I covered for you. Do you think I'm stupid?" She tossed the garbage bag into the dumpster. "What am I saying? Obviously, you *do* think I'm stupid. You took me for a complete sucker or you wouldn't be here tonight."

"What do you mean?" Zack asked nervously.

"What do I *mean*?" Alex asked. She put her hands on her hips. She had unraveled her French braid, and her blond hair was more unruly and curly than ever. Her amber eyes flashed. "You steal a ruby earring at the Met and make nice to me so you can come here to steal the other one—"

"No, I didn't! I swear. Alex, I—"

"Come on, Zack, Mrs. Washburne didn't raise an idiot. I read the description of the thief in the paper. You practically ran out on me at the museum that night, and then you call me up out of nowhere because you want a tour of the kitchen. Then you say you don't mind busing tables! Is this chef gig a good cover for you, or what?"

"Alex, I swear I'm not a thief," Zack said desperately. "Just give me two minutes, and I can explain."

"Why should I?" Alex asked, thrusting her chin at him defiantly. "I hate liars worse than anything."

"Because you must believe somewhere that I'm not a thief, or you wouldn't have covered for me," Zack said.

"I covered for you to save my own neck, buddy," Alex said in a grudging voice. She pushed back the sleeve of her white blouse and looked at her watch.

"What are you doing?" Zack asked nervously.

"Giving you two minutes, bozo," Alex said crisply. "And you just wasted thirty seconds of it."

Zack couldn't help grinning at this feisty girl. But admiring Alex took another ten seconds, and he had no time to waste.

Zack thought fast. He couldn't tell Alex the *complete* truth. That meant he had to confess that not only wasn't he a chef, he was still in high school. He had to improvise. Luckily, for Zack, that was no problem.

"I found the earring in a plate of hors d'oeuvres at the party," he said quickly. "I didn't know who it belonged to, so I was going to call Mrs. Lenihan the next morning to see if she would return it to the owner. I *was* in a hurry that night, but not because I was escaping. But then I got the paper and saw I was a suspect, so I decided it would be easier to just slip it back to her without her noticing. I swear, Alex. I didn't steal it."

Alex stared at him for a long moment. "So are you really a chef?"

Zack nodded. He was afraid that if he admitted that he'd lied about that, Alex would think that he lied about everything.

"Okay," Alex said finally. "I believe you. I might be crazy, but I do."

"Thanks," Zack said. "At least *something* is going right tonight. I'm in worse trouble than ever. Not only did Mrs. Lenihan see me again, but I lost the ruby. There's no way I can give it back to her now."

"I might be able to help you there." Alex dug into the pocket of her black slacks and held up the ruby. "I found it underneath the table." She handed it to Zack. "If you want some advice, I'd say just give it back. I don't know if you'll get another shot at Marion. You freaked her out tonight."

Zack pocketed the ruby. "That's good advice," he admitted. "I'll think about it." But it wasn't just *him* he had to think about. He had to worry about possibly getting the rest of the gang in trouble, too.

Alex looked away. "So I guess you just came here to give back the earring, huh?"

Zack saw a vulnerability in her face he hadn't seen before. It surprised him to see that Alex could look uncertain. But he had a feeling that even if he were to know Alex Washburne for years, she'd still be able to surprise him.

"I *was* worried about the ruby, Alex," he said honestly. "But somehow, all I could think about was you."

Alex turned and looked at him. Slowly, she smiled. "I believe you," she said. "You've got honest eyes, Zack."

That should have made Zack feel great. But somehow, he felt awful. He had to tell her the truth. "Alex—"

"Shhhh." Alex took his hand and pulled him far-ther into the shadows of the alley. A worker came out of the kitchen door and stomped down the steps with two garbage bags. He threw them inside the dumpster and returned wearily to the kitchen.

"You can't stay here," Alex whispered. "We're starting to clean up, and people will be coming out this door."

"But I want to talk to you," Zack said.

Alex frowned, thinking. "A catering firm hired me to be the assistant chef at this big party tomor-row night for some old movie star. It's at the Metro Hotel. Maybe I could get you in."

"The Metro? That's where I'm staying!" Zack exclaimed.

"Perfect," Alex said. "So you'll come?"

"I'll come," Zack promised. Alex was looking at him as though she wouldn't mind if he kissed her. And he wouldn't mind, either. Not a bit. But he couldn't. Not while he was going steady with Kelly. Even if Kelly didn't know, *he* would know. He took her hand and squeezed it instead.

The door opened again, and Alex pointed to the gate at the end of the alley. She put her lips close to his ear. "The gate is open," she whispered. "Go. I'll call you tomorrow afternoon."

Zack nodded and took off. It was hard to leave Alex, but it was now fifteen minutes past curfew. Besides, he didn't want to get her into any more trouble.

As soon as he reached Madison Avenue, he found a cab, and the ride to the hotel was shorter than he'd thought. He would only be twenty minutes late. He hoped the gang had covered for him. Then again, he hoped the gang had missed curfew, too. He'd rather be in trouble with Mr. Loomis than with Kelly!

When he put the key in the lock and opened the door, he was met by five anxious faces. Everyone sprang up and started talking at once.

"Where were you?" Jessie demanded.

"We thought you were arrested!" Lisa exclaimed.

"Do you have the ruby?" Slater asked.

"Did you eat?" Screech questioned.

"I was so worried," Kelly said.

"I'm really sorry, everyone," Zack said. "Is everything cool with Mr. Loomis?"

"We told him you had a stomach flu and were in the bathroom," Slater said. "Screech was in there making barfing noises, so Mr. Loomis left really fast."

"Zack, where *were* you?" Kelly asked.

Zack sank down in an armchair. Suddenly, he felt really tired. It had been quite a night. "I guess I have to come clean," he said. "I had a plan, but I thought I could carry it off without you guys. That way, only one of us would get in trouble if it backfired. I met this chef at the party named Alex Washburne. I found out that Alex worked at the same club Marion belongs to. So when I read in the paper that Marion was throwing a party there, I called Alex and asked if I could come by. I thought I could get to Marion and sneak the ruby earring back in her purse or something. But I blew it."

"You didn't lose the ruby, did you?" Lisa asked.

Zack pulled it out and showed it to them. "No. I dropped it when Marion saw me, but Alex found it and gave it back to me. It was almost a complete disaster."

Kelly sank down on the rug near his feet. "Oh, Zack. You were so brave tonight. And I—" Her lower lip trembled, and her big blue eyes filled with tears.

"Don't cry, Kelly," Zack said. "I'm safe now. I hid behind some garbage cans."

Lisa wrinkled her nose. "We noticed."

"That Alex was a real pal," Slater observed.

"He was awfully nice," Kelly said.

He? Kelly thought Alex was a guy! Zack squirmed uncomfortably. He was used to scheming, but tonight, even he might have stepped over the line. He'd lied to Alex and to Kelly, and Mr. Loomis thought he had a stomach flu. He just hoped he'd see this trip out without being tripped up!

▲   ▼   ▲

The next afternoon, Screech sat alone on a bench in Central Park. After a morning of sightseeing, everyone had split up on mysterious errands. Slater had *said* he was going to the Museum of Modern Art, but who could believe that? And Jessie had headed out later, saying she might meet Slater there. *Yeah, right,* Screech thought. Everyone knew Jessie and Slater couldn't stand to be around each other. Then Kelly had simply disappeared in a cab, and Zack didn't want to leave the hotel until he heard from that Alex fellow.

The only one Screech believed was Lisa. She had gone shopping with Vivian and Daisy. At least he could still depend on *her*.

Even Mr. Loomis was acting weird, Screech thought morosely. He kept canceling all those neat historic trips and scheduling things like roller skating. All week, Screech had been looking forward to this morning's visit to the house where Chester A. Arthur was sworn in as president. But instead, Mr. Loomis had agreed to Ms. McCracken's suggestion to take a Great Pizza Tour of the Upper West Side! What was the world coming to?

Screech had decided that the only thing that could possibly make him feel better would be an afternoon of bird watching in Central Park. But so far the only birds he'd spotted with his binoculars had been pigeons.

Screech looked down the path and let out a groan. Nanny Parker was hurrying toward him.

The sunlight glinted off her glasses, and she was smiling.

"Do you have bat radar or something?" Screech asked her when she came up. "Every time I try to be alone, you show up!"

He expected Nanny to snap back something insulting, but instead, her large brown eyes filled with tears. One tear broke free and trailed down her cheek to drip off her chin onto her I LOVE NEW YORK T-shirt.

Screech was filled with remorse. "Gosh, Nanny, I'm sorry," he said. "I didn't mean to hurt your feelings."

"I thought that maybe you were starting to *like* having me around," Nanny sniffed.

"Well, I am," Screech said. "Sort of."

"Because I really like you," Nanny said in a low voice. "A lot."

"You do?" Screech asked, surprised. Nanny nodded, looking soft and fragile. Suddenly, Screech realized that he'd been telling the truth before. He *was* starting to like having her around. "Would you like to go to the zoo with me?" he blurted.

Nanny beamed at him. "Sure."

That afternoon, Screech got his biggest surprise since his pet hamster Ralph had babies. He had fun with Nanny! She seemed to relax with him for the first time, and she was funny and smart and turned out to love animals just as much as he did. By the time they wandered over to look at the monkeys, Screech started thinking that it might not be too forward to hold her hand.

Would Nanny freak out? Screech tentatively brushed his fingers against hers, and she grabbed his hand tightly and smiled. Screech felt his heart swell. It felt good to have a soft palm nestled against his.

Most of the monkeys were napping in the natural habitat the zoo had created. A wide pool separated them from their human onlookers. Nanny pointed to one monkey who was sunning himself on a rock. "Look at the little guy over there. He's reading the paper!"

Screech laughed. It was true—one of the smaller monkeys had picked up a stray piece of newspaper and was holding it up against his face, as though he were reading it.

"He's probably reading Billy Cahill's column," Nanny said. "I guess that proves that *everybody* in New York does."

Screech raised his binoculars. He adjusted the focus, trying to read the headline. His dad had given him the binoculars for his birthday, and they were super powerful. Suddenly, the picture in the paper swam into focus.

"Oh, my gosh!" he shouted. "It's Sally!"

Chapter 11

▲ ▼ ▲ ▼ ▲ ▼ ▲

"What?" Nanny exclaimed. She jostled his arm. "Let me see."

Screech handed her the binoculars, and she yanked them to her face, nearly strangling him. "That *is* Sally's picture! Could you read the headline?"

"Aaaaggghhh," Screech said.

"Something about the Metro Hotel," Nanny said. She leaned closer to the fence, tightening the strap on Screech's neck even further. "I wonder what it could be."

"Aaaaggghhh," Screech said.

"I hope she didn't have an accident there or something," Nanny said worriedly. She lowered the glasses and looked at Screech. "Are you okay? Your face looks kind of red."

Just then, the monkey looked over at them and bared his teeth, as though their noise was disturbing his reading. Then he threw the paper at them. It caught a gust of wind and sailed over the water and got caught by the fence. Screech snatched it up. Nanny read over his shoulder.

"Oh, my gosh!" she breathed. "Our Sally is Sarah Springer!"

It was true, Screech realized as he rapidly scanned the article. The friend they thought was homeless was the famous actress Sarah Springer who was being honored that very night at the Metro Hotel!

Nanny gazed at Screech with fervent eyes. "Do you know what this *means*, Screech?"

"It means I don't have to worry about Sally anymore," Screech said, still trying to read the article. "Her son Max is pretty rich, so he can take care of her."

Nanny grabbed his arm. "It means that the man she lost, the one who she never told she loved, is Alan Tracy!"

"Alan Tracy? The actor?" Screech said. "He's still really famous. He was just in that movie *Sweet Revenge*. And he got an honorary Oscar last year."

"They acted in five movies together in the forties," Nanny said. "Remember Sally said how she never told him how she felt—she was afraid it would be bad for his career. That's because *her* career started to go downhill then. He's going to be at the party tonight, *and* he's staying at the hotel. He's the man she wanted to see but was afraid to! It all adds up."

"Poor Sally," Screech said. "She must still love him."

Nanny gripped his arm even tighter. "Don't you see what this *means*?"

Screech sighed. "She must be really nervous about seeing him tonight."

"It means I have my scoop!" Nanny exulted.

Slowly, Nanny's words penetrated Screech's brain. "What do you mean?" he asked, dread stealing over him.

"I can leak the story to Billy Cahill," Nanny said rapidly. "I talked to Sally for *hours*. I know how she thinks. She's this big reclusive ex-star who *never* gives interviews, and I *had* one with her! I could even write an article! This could be my big break!"

"But she *didn't* give you an interview," Screech said. "Sally didn't know that you'd find out who she was."

"Well, that's just silly," Nanny said. "She must have figured that we'd find out eventually. She's not exactly invisible, especially with this retrospective of her movies and everything."

"Maybe she told us because she trusted us," Screech said. "She thought we were her friends."

Nanny stared at him. "But don't you see? She's

already getting all this publicity. Why should she care if there's just one more article about her?"

"Because what she told us was *private*!" Screech practically yelled.

Nanny looked at him accusingly. "You're trying to make me feel guilty for just doing my job. I have a responsibility as a journalist, you know."

"You *should* feel guilty," Screech said flatly. "And what do you mean, '. . . have a responsibility as a journalist'? You write a sleazy gossip column for a high school paper!"

Nanny's mouth dropped open. "So that's what you think of me," she said in a choked voice. "Thanks a lot. Don't bother asking me out again, Screech. I never want to see you again!"

Screech watched, stunned, as Nanny started to walk away. "I never even *asked* you out, Nosy Parker!" he bawled after her.

▲   ▼   ▲

Back at the hotel, Zack paced back and forth, staring at the phone. If Alex didn't call, he'd know that she had decided that he was a low-down dirty liar after all. She should have called by now, Zack thought worriedly. It was past three o'clock. She had to tell him if she could get him into the party or not.

Just then, the phone shrilled, and Zack pounced on it. "Hello?"

"Zack, it's Alex. I just called to tell you that my life is falling apart."

"What?" Zack asked, smiling. What a way to begin a conversation! "Alex, what happened?"

A deep sigh came through the receiver. "You know how I'm the assistant chef tonight and it's my big break at the catering firm? Well, the head chef was just rushed to the hospital with appendicitis. I've got to do the whole party by myself!" Alex's voice rose to a wail.

"You can do it, Alex," Zack assured her. "If anyone can pull it off, you can."

"Actually, I was wondering . . ." Alex's voice trailed off. "I know this is awful of me to ask, seeing how you pitched in last night, but . . . Do you think you could help out again?"

"Sure," Zack said. "You want me to bus tables? Pour water? I'm an expert by now."

"I have enough waiters," Alex said. "I need you to cook. Don't worry, the company will pay you. I don't expect you to work for free."

"Cook?" Zack asked in a strangled voice.

"It's a small affair. Only thirty people."

"Cook? Thirty people?" *Do you think they'd like peanut-butter-and-jelly sandwiches?*

"Just hors d'oeuvres. Look, I know it's a lot to ask. But I'd be forever in your debt, Zack. Say yes, please."

Zack gulped. He had to tell her the truth now. It had gone too far. But he thought of Alex's worried voice, and he knew he had to at least try to help her.

Zack crossed his fingers. "Yes," he said.

▲   ▼   ▲

Mitch pulled up at a corner on Park Avenue. He pointed ahead to an imposing apartment house on the corner. "There it is," he said to Kelly.

Kelly leaned over to peer at the building. "Wow," she said.

"You said it," Mitch agreed. "Look, here comes Angela. Right on time."

Kelly looked down the block and saw Angela approaching with a tiny dog that was yapping and snipping at her heels. She turned to Mitch.

"Thank you so much for helping me out, Mitch," she said. "It was really nice of you to call Angela and set this up."

"No problem," Mitch said. "You're in a tough spot." He reached out to touch a lock of Kelly's hair. "And you're a terrific girl."

She smiled into his electric blue eyes. "Thanks."

"I'll wait right here for you," Mitch said.

"You don't have to—"

"I'll be here," Mitch said firmly.

Kelly smiled her thanks and slid out of the cab. Angela handed her the leash. "Here you go. Just tell the doorman you're the new dog walker and you're bringing Pookie up to the Lenihan apartment. The housekeeper is out buying groceries right now. You should have a clear shot."

"You're sure Mrs. Lenihan won't be there?" Kelly asked nervously.

"No way. She's out eating a fifty-dollar lunch of lettuce and designer water. You'll have to take the service elevator. Peons like us don't get to ride with the blue-hairs," Angela said with a smirk. "Good luck. See ya later, Pookie," she said to the dog. "It's been an experience. Hope you choke on a Milk-Bone."

The dog yapped at her, then turned and yapped at Kelly. "Let's go, Pookie," Kelly said.

Everything went like clockwork. The doorman didn't even look twice, just pointed down a hall to the back elevator. Kelly pressed the 6 button, and the door opened right into a pantry off the Lenihan kitchen.

Kelly stepped cautiously inside the kitchen. "Hello?"

No one answered, so she tiptoed out into the hall. Oil paintings lined the wall, and she almost bumped into a marble-topped table. Kelly inched down the hall, peering into various rooms. It was the most beautiful apartment she'd ever seen.

Finally, Kelly pushed open a door and found what must be Marion's bedroom. A rich ruby satin bedspread was on a king-size bed, and hanging over it was an oil painting of a younger Marion. She looked just as cranky twenty years ago, Kelly decided.

Kelly dropped Pookie's leash and tiptoed over to a set of doors in one wall. She opened them and found the biggest closet she'd ever seen. After a moment, she saw that it was highly organized. One part was for day clothes, one for evening clothes. Both parts were organized by color, and on the shelves above the dresses were stacked boxes with labels like BLACK SATIN CHANEL PUMPS or BLUE SILK EVENING PURSE WITH DIAMOND CLASP.

Kelly went directly to the red dresses. She recognized the gown Marion had worn right away, even underneath its plastic garment bag. A card was pinned onto the bag. ACCESSORIES: RUBY EARRINGS, RED SEQUINED PURSE, BLACK PUMPS (SEE BLACK-AND-GOLD SATIN GOWN, CHANEL). Kelly almost giggled. If only Lisa could see this!

She unzipped the bag and carefully took the earring out of her tiny shoulder bag. Kelly nestled the earring into one of the opulent folds of the gold sash of the dress. Then she quickly zipped the bag up, backed out of the closet, and ran out of the bedroom into the hall. Pookie started to yap at her again.

"Shhh," Kelly said, grabbing his leash. She felt so relieved she could almost kiss Pookie.

"Who's that? Is that you, Angela?"

Kelly stopped dead. It was Marion Lenihan! She would recognize that snobby voice anywhere. But she couldn't tell where it was coming from. She had to get to the elevator—and fast.

Kelly dashed down the hall and into the kitchen. She nearly screamed in fright when she saw Marion sitting at the long kitchen counter on a stool, wolfing down a quarter-pounder with cheese and a double order of fries.

Marion began to cough. "You!" she choked. "What are you doing in my house? Did you come back for the other earring?"

"No, I dropped off Pookie," Kelly said.

"Do you expect me to believe that?" Marion said. "You're a thief."

"No, I'm not," Kelly said nervously. "I just wanted to talk to you that night, that's all. I didn't steal your earring. I thought I was related to you. You see, my great-grandfather's name was Lenihan. He came here in the eighteen seventies."

Marion's gaze was frosty. "Are you trying to suggest that we're related, young lady?"

"Well, I *did* wonder about it," Kelly said. "Do you have an ancestor named Andrew Lenihan?"

Marion sniffed. "He was my grandfather's brother. A bohemian. He never made a penny in his life. He died in the Spanish-American War, the old fool. So if you're thinking that being distantly related to him means you're entitled to one penny of the Lenihan money, you can think again!"

"I wasn't thinking about the money," Kelly said. "I just wanted to know."

"Sure," Marion said, reaching for the phone. "Now you can think about it while you're in jail."

Kelly thought she would pass out. She'd never been so frightened. If only Zack were here! He could talk his way out of anything.

But wasn't it time, Kelly thought, she stopped depending on Zack?

"Okay, call the police," Kelly said crisply. "And I'll give the press a nice interview from the station all about how I'm related to you."

"No one will believe you," Marion scoffed.

"And I'll tell them how we discussed it while you were scarfing down a quarter-pounder with cheese." Kelly said. "Funny how the most famous gourmet vegetarian in New York sneaks hamburgers while her housekeeper is out buying sprouts. I bet Billy Cahill would be glad to hear about *that*. It would make such a funny column! Can't you just see everybody laughing over their coffee tomorrow morning?"

Marion hesitated. Then she slowly replaced the phone.

"And another thing," Kelly said. "If I were you, I'd search a little harder for that earring. You might find out that you had it all the time." Letting go of Pookie's leash, she started toward the elevator. "See you, *Auntie* Marion!"

Kelly hit the elevator button. She gave one last

glance back at Marion and burst out laughing. Poor
Marion wouldn't even get to finish her hamburger.
Pookie had downed it in one bite!

▲   ▼   ▲

When Mitch and Kelly pulled up in front of the
hotel, they saw Zack, Lisa, Slater, and Jessie standing outside in a tight circle, talking.

"I can't wait to tell them," Kelly said, springing
out of the cab. She ran toward them. "Guess what!
I returned the ruby! We're off the hook!"

Zack looked shocked. "You *what*?"

Kelly frowned. Did he have to be so surprised?
But then everyone started asking her questions at
once, and Kelly had to tell the gang the whole story
from the beginning. "I couldn't have done it without Mitch," she finished.

"Mitch?" Zack asked. He saw a great-looking
guy get out of a cab and start toward them. He was
taller than Zack. He was older. He was better looking. Even his jeans fit better. *This* was Kelly's
"nice" cabdriver? He looked at her, and she
blushed and dropped her eyes.

"Well, that's one problem down," Lisa said.
"But we still have another one, Kelly. You know the
chef Zack met? Well, Alex asked Zack to help out
with the party tonight. Zack is supposed to *cook*!"

"Alex still thinks you're a chef?" Kelly asked. "Why don't you just tell him the truth?"

"I can't," Zack said. "Trust me on that. But even if I could, I don't want to. I *want* to help out. I owe Alex."

"Well, what are we going to do?" Kelly asked. "Between all of us, we could probably microwave some popcorn, but I don't think that will do it."

"That's the problem," Lisa said grimly.

"I have an idea," Mitch said. "New York is the greatest city in the world for takeout, and I know all the best places. *And* I can get you the best deals."

"Takeout is expensive, no matter what," Kelly said worriedly.

"No problem," Zack said. "Alex gave me a check for my services. I wasn't going to cash it, but I might as well. I can do it at the hotel desk. Then we'll have money to buy food. But we only have twenty minutes."

Mitch pointed to his cab. "Then we'd better get moving. My chariot awaits!"

Chapter 12

▲ ▼ ▲ ▼ ▲ ▼ ▲

Somehow, they fought the traffic, rude counterpersons, and the clock—and they did it. They bought a delicious assortment of food, from miniature enchiladas stuffed with crabmeat to cheese popovers. Mitch pulled up to the hotel's back entrance, and Zack hefted the shopping bags and dashed into the hotel kitchen. Alex had already arranged with the hotel staff to borrow a corner of the kitchen for the party.

Zack asked the hotel cook how to turn on the oven. He put in the enchiladas and the popovers to warm, then slid the cold salads into the huge refrigerator to keep cool. Alex was due to arrive any minute, and she'd think he had been working for hours.

Lisa poked her head in the kitchen. "The people are starting to arrive," she said.

From behind her, the crew from the catering company began to stagger in, their arms full of platters of food. Alex followed, looking professional in her black pants and white shirt.

"Zack!" she cried. "Thanks for coming. Is everything under control?"

"Hi, Alex," Zack said. "All set."

Lisa looked at Zack, then at Alex. *Alex is a girl!* she thought. *So that's why Zack's been so mysterious lately.* Maybe she should stick around and see what was going on. Lisa considered hiding, but Alex and Zack only had eyes for each other.

"Let me see what you made," Alex said to Zack as she tied an apron around her waist. "I'm sure it's delicious."

"I have some things in the oven, keeping warm," Zack said. "Let me tell you, it was a job to pull this together."

"I know it must have been," Alex said as she opened the oven. She peered inside.

"Crab enchiladas and cheese popovers," Zack said.

Alex hesitated a long moment. Then she turned around casually. "What kind of cheese?"

Darn. Zack couldn't remember. "Swiss," he guessed. It was the only thing he could think of besides Cheez Whiz.

"Mmmm," Alex said. "What else did you make?"

"Some cold salads in the fridge."

Alex opened the fridge and peeked at the salads.

"Mmmm," she said again. "Oh—jicama."

"Do you have the hiccups?" Zack said. "I always get them when I'm nervous."

"*Hic-a-ma,*" Alex repeated. "In the salad. Where did you get that jicama? It's out of season."

"I have my ways," Zack said. He wondered what the heck *hic-a-ma* was.

Alex crossed her arms. "Zack, remember how I told you that I believed that you weren't a liar?"

"Of course," Zack said.

"I take it back. These whoppers could outdo Burger King. Jicama is *not* out of season. Not that you even *know* what jicama is. The popovers are filled with goat cheese, not Swiss. And if you're going to buy takeout food and pass it off as your own, the *least* you can do is not go to the company I work for and buy my very own crab enchiladas!"

"Oops," Zack said.

"Oops is right, pal," Alex said. "'Fess up. You're either a bad chef, a lousy con man, or an incompetent jewel thief. Or maybe you're all three."

"Actually, I'm a high school student," Zack said. "I'm here on my senior class trip. And everything I told you about the earring was true, except that it didn't fall into a plate of hors d'oeuvres. It fell into my friend Lisa's purse."

Alex sighed. "So why did you lie?"

"Because I wanted to get to know you better," Zack said softly. "But I guess I blew it."

"You sure did," Alex said. "Look, Zack. I can't hate you. You seem like a really nice guy. But I could never trust you again."

Zack had thought that there could never be a situation that he couldn't talk his way out of. Now he knew there was. He nodded sadly. "I know. I'm really sorry, Alex."

Zack *did* look really sorry, Lisa saw. As a matter of fact, he looked crushed. And she could swear that even though Alex seemed cool, she was trying not to cry.

"Apology accepted," Alex said, quickly turning her back on Zack and fussing with a tray of food. "Now, if you don't mind, I have work to do."

▲   ▼   ▲

Screech sneaked into the party and stationed himself in a quiet corner by the entrance. He didn't see Sally, but he figured she was in one of the inner rooms, where most of the party had gathered. The only people in the first room were waiters, who were putting the finishing touches on the long buffet table.

Screech stood, ready for action. He wasn't sure *what* action, but he knew if Billy Cahill poked his nose in, he'd get it bopped. There was no way Screech would let Sally be hurt.

The door opened, and a group of well-dressed people poured in, laughing and talking. They made their way to the inner room, but a slight figure separated herself from them and hung back. It was Nanny. She was dressed in a sea green dress, and if Screech hadn't been so furious at her, he'd have admitted that she looked pretty.

She saw him, and her steps faltered. Then her shoulders set determinedly, and she walked over. "I was looking for you," she said.

"Don't try to distract me," Screech said, keeping his eye on the door. "If I see your friend Billy Cahill come through that door, I'm tackling him."

"Billy Cahill won't be coming, Screech," Nanny said.

"Why not?" Screech asked. "Wasn't your scoop big enough for him?"

"I didn't tell him," Nanny said. "I didn't tell anybody. I'll *never* tell anybody what Sally told us. You were right, Screech. Sally is our friend, and I have no right to do it."

"Oh," Screech said. He felt like the wind had been taken right out of his sails. "What made you change your mind?"

"You did," Nanny said simply. "Look, Screech, I don't have any friends. I moved to Palisades from Ohio in the middle of my junior year. Everybody was already friends with somebody. I was really shy about meeting people, too."

"How could someone who talks so much be shy?" Screech asked.

"I talk a lot because I'm nervous," Nanny said. "I started the column in the *Beacon* because I thought it might help me make friends. Instead, I just made enemies. Then I told myself I didn't care. But I *do* care. I want to be like you, Screech. I want to be a good friend," Nanny finished in a small voice. "I want to learn how."

A voice rose up from a deep armchair behind them. The chair's back was to them, so they hadn't seen anyone sitting in it. "I think you already know, dear."

"Sally!" Nanny gasped.

Slowly, Sally stood up and came around the armchair to face them. She was no longer dressed in baggy khaki pants and sneakers. She was wearing a silk black trouser suit and a white satin blouse, and tiny pearl earrings were in her ears. Her hair was in its usual style, pulled straight back, but it was twisted in an elegant bun.

She smiled. "I always hated parties. I was hiding out. I didn't mean to eavesdrop."

"Sometimes you can't help it," Nanny agreed.

"Thank you for not telling anyone my story, Nanny," Sally said. "I didn't think you kids would recognize an old fogy like me."

"You're not an old fogy," Screech said. "You're beautiful."

Sally laughed. "I should definitely keep you around, Samuel."

"Did you see Alan?" Nanny asked breathlessly.

Sally nodded. "We're having a late supper together later," she said. "I think we have a lot to talk over." She leaned over and whispered, "Don't tell anyone."

"I won't," Nanny promised fervently.

Sally put her hands on their shoulders. "So, now that everything's out in the open, I'd like both of you to stay and enjoy the party. And I'd also like to thank you for being such good friends to me. If there's ever anything I can do for you, just let me know."

Screech hesitated. Suddenly, he had a brainstorm. "As a matter of fact . . ."

▲   ▼   ▲

Kelly pushed open the front door of the hotel, a plate of food in her hands for Mitch. After he'd gone to so much trouble, he deserved a free meal. She'd gone to the kitchen to ask Zack if there was extra food, but he hadn't been there. Instead, a pretty blond chef had filled up a plate for her as soon as she'd heard Kelly was a friend of Zack's. Kelly had no idea why the girl had given her a funny look. Maybe she had never met a Californian before.

Kelly hurried toward Mitch's cab, but when she got there, she realized he wasn't in it. Where could he have gone? Kelly wondered. Now his enchiladas would get cold.

She turned around, frowning, and at that moment, Mitch came out of the hotel. He ran toward her, his face alight. He reached her and swept her up in his arms. The paper plate flew out of Kelly's hands and landed upside down in the gutter.

"Mitch!" Kelly protested, laughing. "You just trashed your dinner!"

"Who cares!" Mitch said, stepping back and throwing his arms up in the air. "Kelly, the most amazing thing just happened. Your friend Screech ran out here to get me and brought me inside to the party!"

"Sarah Springer's party?" Kelly asked. "But how did Screech get in?"

"He knows Sarah," Mitch said. "That is, he didn't *know* that he knew her, but he knew her."

"What?"

"It's not important. You can ask him the whole story later. The important thing is, Sarah took me over to her son and introduced me! I met Max Springer, Kelly!"

"That's wonderful!" Kelly exclaimed. "Oh, Mitch, you got exactly what you wanted."

Mitch started to pace. "He's casting his new play. And he asked me to audition! He says I have the right look for a supporting role. He says it's not big, but it's important. It's a star-maker role, Kelly."

"Do you think you'll get it?" Kelly asked.

Mitch whirled around. "I'll give it my best shot," he said fiercely.

"Oh, Mitch, I'm so happy for you," Kelly said. "We've got to celebrate."

"Celebrate? I don't have time," Mitch said flatly. "The audition is Wednesday. I've got to prepare. I've got to figure out what monologue I want to do. I've got to rehearse it. I'm going to be busy every single minute until Wednesday."

"Oh," Kelly said. "I'm leaving Sunday. I guess I won't see you again."

"I'm going to ask Presley to help me decide on which monologue to do," Mitch said, starting to pace again. "And Nancy is really good at constructive criticism." He turned to face her. "You know, none of this would have happened without you, Kelly. You're my good luck charm."

Even though she was hurt that Mitch hadn't paid attention when she said when she'd be leaving, Kelly softened. "I'm glad," she said.

He leaned forward and kissed her. "Have a good trip home," he said. "And if you're ever in New York again, look me up."

Kelly gave a faint smile. "You'll probably be famous by then."

He flashed her a cocky grin. "I hope so. But I'll never forget you, Kelly."

"And I'll never forget you," Kelly answered. It was true. Mitch had showed her a whole new world. She'd fantasized about being part of it someday. Maybe it was just a dream. But it had been fun to dream it.

Mitch gave her a last wave, then headed for his cab. Kelly sighed and leaned against the hotel building. She had come close to falling for Mitch. But wasn't it lucky that he turned out to be too ambitious to fall in love? She was going steady with Zack. She felt guilty enough as it was.

Lisa came out of the hotel and saw her. "Did you find Mitch?" she asked.

Kelly nodded. "He just took off. He said goodbye. Oh, Lisa, I feel so guilty. How could I have fallen for another guy, even for three days? Zack is the most wonderful boyfriend in the world. I feel like I've betrayed him!"

"Mmmm," Lisa said. "I wouldn't feel *too* guilty if I were you."

Kelly turned. "What are you talking about?"

"Well, let's just say that while you've been with Mitch, Zack's been busy. Did you know that the chef Alex Washburne is a girl? A very pretty girl, with blond curly hair."

"*That's* Alex Washburne?" Kelly gasped. "Why did Zack let us think she was a guy?"

"For the same reason you didn't want Zack to go to that party last night," Lisa responded. "Don't worry, though. Alex just blew Zack off because he lied to her about being a chef."

"Oh, Lisa," Kelly said with a sigh. "What's going to happen with Zack and me? I really *do* love him."

"I know you do," Lisa said gently. "But just because you love each other doesn't mean you can't be attracted to other people."

"I guess not," Kelly agreed sadly. "This trip sure proved it."

She shivered. The sun was sinking below the gray skyscrapers, and suddenly she felt cold. When she had thought about the class trip back in Palisades, she'd fantasized about plenty of romantic times with Zack. Instead, they'd both had their most romantic moments with other people. Did they have a future together at all?

▲   ▼   ▲

On Sunday morning, the lobby was chaos as the class struggled with their luggage and Mr. Loomis tried to take a head count.

"Everybody, stand still!" he barked, and everyone froze. He counted heads quickly, then said, "All right, you can move. But don't go anywhere!"

"I hate to say it, but I'll be glad to get home," Zack told Kelly. "I feel like I need a vacation after this vacation."

"I know what you mean," Kelly said. She still felt a little awkward with Zack. She knew that he knew about Mitch. And by now, he must know that she knew about Alex. But neither one of them wanted to talk about it.

"Well, I had a great time," Jessie said happily. "And the last two days were the best of all."

"The best," Slater agreed. He winked at her. They'd managed to steal away yesterday for a long, romantic walk.

"Hey, Nanny," Zack said. "Slater and Jessie agreed on something. You might want to print it in the *Bayside Beacon*."

"No way," Nanny said with a grin. "Anything I hear from you guys is strictly off-limits. And I'm not going to report gossip anymore. Only *news*. I think I've finally learned the difference."

Suddenly, Zack heard Ms. McCracken's voice above the crowd. "What do you mean, I sent you chocolates?" she asked.

"Uh-oh," Zack said under his breath. He backed up until he was leaning against the wall. Around the corner, Ms. McCracken and Mr. Loomis were arguing in low voices.

"Don't be shy, Maisie," Mr. Loomis said. "I was really touched. That's the first time I thought of you as anything other than an annoying crank."

"A *crank*?" Maisie McCracken gasped.

"I don't think that any*more*," Mr. Loomis said

quickly. "The chocolates showed me that you really are sensitive and sweet. I admit I was a little shocked to be courted by a woman, but actually, it was kind of fun."

"I didn't *give* you any chocolates," Ms. McCracken said. "*You're* the one who courted *me*. What about those roses?"

Mr. Loomis frowned. "I never sent you roses."

"And that note? You said that you realized that you came off like a stuffy jerk," Ms. McCracken continued.

"A stuffy jerk?" Mr. Loomis said, shocked. "That's ridiculous!"

"Not at all," Ms. McCracken said. "I'm beginning to see how very true it *is*."

"I never sent you that note!" Mr. Loomis said.

"And I never sent you chocolates!"

There was a long pause.

"Wait a second here," Mr. Loomis said. "A light is beginning to dawn. If we're both telling the truth, who's the one who's been promoting this romance?"

"It has to be one of the students," Ms. McCracken said.

Zack started to sidle away. He knew that it wouldn't take Mr. Loomis and Ms. McCracken long to put two and two together and point the finger at the scam-meister of Bayside High. *If* they could find him.

"Zack?" Kelly came over and peered at him. "Are you okay? You look kind of pale."

"Fine," Zack said. "I was just wondering, Kelly. Has anyone ever spent a five-hour flight to California in the rest room?"

Don't miss the next  HOT novel about the "SAVED BY THE BELL" gang

THAT OLD ZACK MAGIC

Zack dares Mario to spend the night alone at Bayside—and suddenly the whole gang's in on the idea. After all, nobody wants to miss out on getting to the bottom of all the mysterious things that have been happening at Bayside recently.

Meanwhile, Lisa's love life is fizzling. It seems that her super-hunk boyfriend, Cal Everhart, has eyes for her adorable new neighbor!

Will Zack and the gang uncover the truth? Will Lisa lose Cal forever? Find out in the next "Saved by the Bell" novel!